T0195578

PNEUMA

DR. NEETHA JOSEPH

BALBOA.
PRESS

A DIVISION OF HAY HOUSE

Balboa Press books may be ordered through booksellers or by contacting:

Balboa Press
A Division of Hay House
1663 Liberty Drive
Bloomington, IN 47403
www.balboapress.com
1 (877) 407-4847

Print information available on the last page.

ISBN: 978-1-5043-0959-2 (sc)
ISBN: 978-1-5043-0960-8 (e)

Balboa Press rev. date: 07/24/2017

Dedicated to my father P.C. Joseph, my beloved mother Alphy Joseph and my adorable son Jerry Melvin

CONTENTS

Chapter 1   Enigmas.. 1

Chapter 2   A Stab in the Back 9

Chapter 3   Hurdles 19

Chapter 4   Purloined.. 27

Chapter 5   Voices from the past... 37

Chapter 6   Shadows... 45

Chapter 7   Hunted.. 55

Chapter 8   Reminiscences 65

Chapter 9   Crumbled.. 75

Chapter 10   Departed... 83

Chapter 11   Thorns of Life 87

Chapter 12   Perquisition 95

ONE

ENIGMAS

Neha sensed a slow movement around her, which could have been easily mistaken for a gentle breeze, had it not begun to seep through her. She felt like she was being possessed by an unknown entity and she stiffened when the unexplainable assumed the shape or form of a hand that began to fondle her. She resisted with her will as she was incapable of pushing the invisible force away from her. Fear paralysed her as the thought that she was becoming one with the supernatural invaded her mind, which commenced a bout of incessant chanting. Prayers seemed to be powerless in the face of that mystifying persistent potency which continued to maraud against her will.

Fingers trailed on her supple skin and Neha could hear her deafeningly loud breathing drown every other sound in her bedroom.

She could not summon enough courage to open her eyes let alone sit up and investigate or reason the origin of the unexpected intrusion that was frighteningly and strangely seductive. She was unsuccessful in her rationalisation as the roving hand was determined to terminate her digressions and left her gasping in pleasure. Manipulative fingers prodding, probing and caressing her body from head to toe made it impossible for her to harbour any sinister feelings about the freakish encounter.

The inscrutable turned more demanding and urgent, which matched Neha's rapid breathing, forcing her to relax and subduing her instinct to protest. She could feel its grip tightening around her waist groping for softness embedded within her inner lips. When she struggled to appear unresponsive, Neha felt the hold slacken only to wander away to the soft swell that accentuated her femininity. Hungrily the hand clenched and unclenched over her mounds of softness making her arching body clamour for more. Neha suppressed her moans as disturbing John, who was sleeping in the adjacent room, was unthinkable during the witching hours.

Wave after wave of sensual pleasure washed over her ruining the possibility of peaceful repose, which would have rejuvenated her for the next day's tedious hours. Neha's attempts to surface from the tormenting sea of desires were shattered when the caresses turned into agonisingly slow penetration that engulfed her entire being in sweet ache. She quivered with delight unable to deduce the source of her enjoyment. She relished the moment when her inner lips parted welcoming the anticipated thrust wishing for the incessant tease and torment to consume her with a raging passion. She felt a tug at her fuller bottom lip and as she was succumbing to the bewitchment a melodious ascending ringtone ended the night of clandestine debauchery.

Neha switched off the alarm on her mobile phone and lay staring at the ceiling struggling to differentiate between fantasy and reality. The nightmarish dream felt so real that it was impossible to dismiss it as chimera. She headed for the showers not wanting to break working days' routine and as she unwound herself in the long warm shower she reflected on how life itself was an enigma. There were so many occurrences in her life that would have appeared less abstruse had she been successful in obtaining solutions. With a sigh, Neha concluded her reminiscences as the call of duty claimed her mornings. Ensuring that John woke up on time, showered, changed in to full school uniform and had a healthy breakfast took a toll on her and by the time she hit the road she found herself ranting and raving about innumerable issues such as lack of discipline, traffic and lateness.

Neha dropped John at his high school as usual and breathed a sigh of relief only when she had eluded the traffic bottleneck near the school zone. The smoothing vehicular flow of the Hume Highway, which was uninterrupted, untangled Neha's taut nerves and she paid some attention to Mikee and Emma's Radio show on 96.1. It usually took an hour's drive to get to her destination and as she was driving Neha thought that her decision to migrate to Australia in her advanced stages of pregnancy throwing away a substantive position in a government institution was nothing short of a gamble. She was one of the fortunate candidates, among the several hundred thousand who sat for the Teacher's Recruitment Board examination, to have emerged victorious both in the written section and the interview. Within few months, Neha received the guaranteed permanent appointment letter as lecturer in English at a Government Arts College and Neha's teaching career skyrocketed with the transition from self-financing institutions to government colleges. Industriousness being her middle name she laboured for four years to complete her doctoral thesis on existentialism, however, its submission was followed by the Australian government's grant of Permanent Resident visa at an hour that was fortuitous.

Neha realised the need to focus on the road as her musings were impairing her driving skills. She swerved dangerously around the corner of Charming Rd and into the teachers' parking lot ignoring the 40kms school zone sign. As she rushed into the school building, she noticed mothers with prams and fathers in work attire waiting outside the library.

'It must be one of those PTA meetings,' Neha ruminated as she stormed into the staffroom flinging a muffled 'Good morning' to the occupants engrossed with their routines.

She breathed a sigh of relief when she noticed a blank, highlighted space on her timetable for period 1. Pangs of hunger ravaging her reminded Neha that she had skipped breakfast. Coffee was inevitable, of course! As she watched the thin group of mothers with prams and toddlers grow into a significant cluster in the quad through the staffroom window, Neha envisioned the days when she traversed everywhere with a pram. Commuting to University was no different.

Recollections of sprinting with the pram to drop her baby off at the University Kids campus and having to retrace the route to attend lectures; of facing disappointments when assignments were returned sans credit or distinction and of being a victim to tall poppy's syndrome; of exiting the lecture hall just before 7 pm to pick her son from the day care at closing time and of wondering, while looking at the tear-stained face of a traumatised child who had lost his battle to exhaustion, if the sacrifice made for a tertiary qualification was worth the grief, inundated her psyche. Recollections of pushing a pram in the early hours of the morning through the nearly deserted streets of Campsie; of quickening pace to reach the residence of a family day carer who defied rules to welcome a struggling migrant's nine months old baby at the crack of dawn; of whizzing through Beamish Street and boarding a specific train to ascertain that Kuring-gai campus was reached on time via linking transportation came crowding into her mind.

Neha, who was never a quitter, knew only too well that adversities often lead to accolades. She persevered holding on to moments such as a rare display of genuine affection by a few friends who claimed her succinct spare time, a word of recognition that augmented her sense of achievement, a goal-intoxicated contribution that would eventually warrant success. With great reluctance, she yanked her gaze from the quad reminding herself of the need to organise herself for the next period. As she ascended the stairs, the day appeared ominous for some awful reason. She could not dismiss the foreboding feeling as insignificant. It dampened her high spirits and wrenched away her moment of basking in the glory of her accomplishments.

She shoved the anxiety building within her to the back of her mind and concentrated on distributing workbooks to Year 8 students who had piled into the classroom at the knell of the bell. She was kept on toes by the queries of inquisitive children whose lively expressions betrayed their growing interest in the topic 'Media Madness', which they were determined to mask. It was their way of seeking vengeance on an educator, who did not believe in wasting a minute of their lesson in frivolous pursuits. Applying themselves diligently through any learning activity for more than half a lesson was sheer injustice to them. Being an experienced teacher, Neha was not fooled by their counterfeit disinterest. In fact, they were so skilled at their pretensions that their histrionics would have fetched them Oscar nominations. She carried on unperturbed and strained to suppress her amusement, which was short-lived due to an unforeseen interruption.

Neha was relieved by a faculty member from her lesson as the Deputy Principal had to discuss a matter of utmost significance with her. Once again that daunting feeling pervaded her entire being. It travelled languidly like a slow poison making each step to the DP's office more arduous.

When she eventually made it to the office, the DP said, 'Close the door. I received this complaint this morning. Take a seat. I want you to read it before I can talk to you about the next step.'

As her eyes skimmed and scanned through the sheets, the words mocked her so derisively. Her co-worker's false allegations paralysing every nerve in her body, reducing her to a state of immobility.

'This is not true. I have not spread rumours about anyone. Some of the information in the document did not happen. It's just plain lies,' said Neha in an almost hysterical voice when she finished reading the document.

'Where is the evidence? No names have been mentioned. I want those nameless students to be brave enough to say things to my face,' added Neha passionately.

Her request for attestation only extorted a, 'There will be a meeting tomorrow morning and you are allowed to bring a fed rep for support.'

Neha forced herself to exit the DP's office and walked through the corridor to the English staffroom with a heavy heart. Sadness overwhelmed her as the realisation, that a conspiracy had been hatched, dawned on her. Careless comments made about colleagues had been twisted and manipulated by the anonymous conspirators to suit their purpose. What brought tears to her eyes was the unfair manner, in which the issue had been dealt. Neha had no say in the matter with her request for proof fallen on deaf ears. Why a casual teacher was given undue importance and a permanent staff stripped of her dignity was an enigma! Not that Neha wanted any staff in tentative positions to be treated without equity. She was determined to expose the falsity behind the accusations, however, as she read and re-read the document to type up a counter response, uncontrollable sobs shook her body. The whole affair was inequitable as there had been many instances of unprofessional conduct displayed by the casual staff towards Neha including deliberate swearing and an insincere apology to mask insolence.

Amidst her sobbing, Neha wondered if her procrastination had turned the tables around. She should have gathered evidence and reported unprofessional conduct of the casual staff early on instead of ignoring rudeness and disrespect. Under the circumstances, Neha speculated, if things would have been favourable for her even if she had made the first move. The perception that she would have been victimised either way fetched a relentless downpour of tears. The screen before Neha became a blur and she realised she was not in a state of mind to continue. She was decisive about not teaching any more classes that day. Intending to cause no more damage to the situation, especially before the meeting, Neha packed her things quickly before students pried her with questions about her red eyes. She was not fortunate in avoiding detection. By the time she had reached the teacher's car park, students who were concerned about her distressed state and who had a whiff of what had occurred, arrived at their own conclusions.

While a storm brewed within Neha, the world continued calmly with her chores. An hour later, she stared with satisfaction at what she had typed in response to the false allegations. The compositional process had a soothing effect as it allowed her to unburden her yoke with each upright word saluting her righteousness. Neither did the incident kill Neha nor did it make her strong. She became imperceptible. The more she ventured through the wilderness of life the more secretive she became. An invisible warrior.

TWO

A STAB IN THE BACK

Two decades ago, when Neha was looking forward to graduate Master's degree with flying colours, when romance inspired her to defy society, traditions and culture; when rebellion dictated her choices and decisions, she was subjected to an undesirable interview. An interview, where she was forced to eat the humble pie in the presence of the institution's correspondent Mrs. Chandra and her father, where she had no other alternative but to swallow the insults that struggled to find its way out and where she had to take an oath to disown her boyfriend despite the fact she was twenty-two years of age. P.S.G.R Krishnammal college for women, Coimbatore was one of the best in the industry and prided itself for inculcating cultural values in its students. To turn a blind eye to a defiant postgraduate catholic student roaming the streets of the city with a Hindu boy on a motorbike would not only tarnish the reputation of the esteemed institution that values discipline above all things but also that of the student, whose chastity would be questionable in the marriage market.

Realising that Vincent was silent during Mrs. Chandra's accusations she said, 'Looks like you have no problem with your daughter going around so openly with her boyfriend. Maybe you have ulterior motives in allowing her to gallivant.'

'I have not allowed her a boyfriend. I did not know she was seeing him until you brought it to my notice,' Vincent replied calmly but sounded unhappy.

'I want a written agreement from Neha that she will not have any interaction with the 'so-called' boyfriend before we conclude this interview,' said Mrs. Chandra to Vincent who was looking at his tightly clasped hands resting on his lap.

After pausing for a few seconds, she added, 'Refusal to oblige with the stipulations would be met with expulsion.'

'I will give it in writing,' consented Neha as she did not want to prolong the humiliation her father was subjected to through no fault of his own.

She signed the written agreement in silence and recorded a stranger's name on the blank where she was supposed to include her boyfriend's name. Oblivious to her deviousness, Mrs. Chandra accepted the agreement with a triumphant smile. The chastisement at the interview ended with just a warning as the institution had great expectations from Neha, a prospective university rank holder. When Neha walked out of the correspondent's office that day she was determined more than ever to continue her affair and to seek employment further away from home on the completion of the course.

Neha reasoned that with employment came economic independence and freedom of choice. Since the interview, both Stella and Vincent tried everything in their capacity to talk Neha out of her relationship with Prem. Falling a victim to their warped logic and brainwashing was out of question. She wasted no time in applying for teaching positions in residential schools and was successful in her endeavours at KTS, Pollachi, a town approximately 44kms away from her hometown. The offer of employment was lucrative as Neha was offered free boarding and lodging besides a reasonable monthly salary. It was an escape ticket to paradise; a paradise where endless harangue on ingratitude, social expectations, failure of inter-caste marriages etc. would not be delivered periodically; a paradise where Neha would be her own master and which would be immune to parental control.

The school was situated in the heart of the residential area of Vasanthi Nagar, which could be reached via Malingapuram, a rich suburban area with palatial homes lining both the sides of wide tarred roads. The female correspondent of the school, Mrs. Kalinga who was a tall, graceful, eloquent and well-built lady, was a strict task master. Neha's memory of the first day talk given to the newly appointed residential staff was still vivid. She commenced with housekeeping, teacher's uniform, which was blue blouse and blue plain saree, and proceeded to talk about the neighbourhood.

Mrs. Kalinga added as an afterthought, 'You would have noticed on your way here that the neighbourhood is unusually quiet. This is how it is on most days,' to which most of the residential staff nodded in accordance.

'Residential staff are advised not to go for outing in uniform as the local community would recognise which school you represent. If you're using public transportation, it is recommended that you hire an auto rickshaw to reach school instead of choosing to walk alone through the wide streets of Malingapuram,' continued Mrs. Kalinga.

The talk ended with emphasis on the importance of lesson preparations and meeting deadlines.

Neha was accommodated with five other inexperienced teachers in a dormitory with few two-tier beds and an attached toilet. It was a whole new world for her with new friends and new found independence. The dining room, which was adjacent to the dormitory, wafted out delicious aroma four times a day and became a favourite hangout for all the residential staff. During one of the exchanges, Neha learnt about the huge influx of newly appointed fresh graduates every year and wondered the cause for their voluntary or involuntary resignation. She pushed the thought to the back of her mind as the novelty of the place had a strange appeal, which fulfilled her soul-sapping mind that desperately longed for a refreshing change.

Brilliant, excited faces of uniformed boys and girls swam before Neha's eyes and their polite greeting, which had a curiously intoxicating effect, made her feel important. Even though she basked in the glory of the sudden attention she was receiving from intrusive students, not once did she forget that she was in a socially responsible position. Her popularity grew with the school community's increased confidence in her abilities and with her newly acquired friends. Secrets were shared, jokes were cracked, free food critiqued, school administration criticised and there was consensus on everything that was bartered.

There was a time of dissent when Neha was not worldly wise to feign ignorance, to steer herself away from flaunting her knowledge on functional grammar and to stop herself from proving a figure of authority, Mrs. Kalinga, incorrect. Every expression left an impression. Mrs. Kalinga stubbornly adopted the path of stony silence refusing to acknowledge Neha's presence. As Neha was offended, she evaded the correspondent's company in ingenious ways. On reflection, Neha found the silent drama between them hilarious but was forced to admit that it was the only way escalation of conflict could have been prevented.

Neha looked forward to weekends with anticipation and excitement as Prem picked her up at the gates of the school. It was hard to hide the pleasure of seeing each other after a week's separation as they stood grinning at each other for no explicable reason. After an hour's ride to a picturesque place, less frequented by people, they shared the week's occurrences, whispered endearments and found pleasure in stolen kisses. Contended in each other's company they continued their journey to their hometown. Prem dropped Neha off in her neighbourhood on Friday evenings and picked her up on Sunday evenings when the couple got yet another opportunity to indulge in amorous behavior, which assisted them through another week's disconnection.

The weekend meetings were not always romantic and predictable. Engrossed in conversation, Neha failed to notice the deliberate deviation made by the lorry driver who came in the opposite direction. However, Prem's swift reflexes averted what could have been a tragic death or fatal accident. He veered sharply into the bushes that lined either sides of the national highway; the tyres skidded throwing Neha off the bike into the bushes. Prem, on the other hand, fell heavily on his left shoulder, sideways, with the weight of the bike on his left leg as he was still clutching the handles tightly to balance the two-wheeler. For a minute, Neha lay dazed in the bushes but Prem's concerned voice brought her out of the state of shock. It was his frantic comment that made Neha realise that her black churidhar was covered with thorns and when she attempted to stand erect, pain seared through her palms with which she had balanced her unforeseen plummet, and her knees.

There was no time to waste and together they hurriedly removed the thorns as Prem did not want Neha's parents to learn about the accident. He did not want to add fuel to the fire. He could almost sense the hostility of her parents as he was the negative influence who beguiled their dutiful daughter and transformed her into an uncontrollable wretch. When he started the bike, and operated the clutch lever he was doubtful about dismissing the ache in his shoulder as an insignificant injury that would not require medical attention.

On her return journey to school, Neha was distraught to hear Prem say, 'I had to consume pain killers to get through the weekend. I have booked an appointment with a specialist to find out the severity of the damage.'

'Hope it does not require surgery. Do you think the accident was a deliberate hit and run?' asked Neha sounding a little distressed.

'Don't know. I have something to show you. It is a newspaper cutting of an article about missing teenage girls and young women in Pollachi. I just want you to be careful. Have a read,' said Prem handing the piece of paper to her.

According to the article, rumours were rife that the missing girls were forced into sexual acts before they were trafficked or murdered by an anonymous notorious group of influential people who produced blue films. The article's reference to Mahabalipuram, which sounded like Malingaparam, the suburb through which most residential staff made their way to the public transport depot for further travel, failed to quell a queer fear that was building within her. Her mind worked faster than lightning associating the correspondent's warning about walking through the streets of

Malingapuram and the unusual inflow and outflow of young staff every year with the atrocities delineated in the article.

When she reached her dormitory, she was introduced to a new staff and roommate, Catherine, who unable to withstand the pressures correlated with the executive positions in the corporate world, switched professions. Although Neha found the reason guileful, she extended her warm welcome. She lost no time in discussing the article with her roommates when Catherine was in the shower.

'There is something strange going on in this place. What made the teachers who were appointed last year leave? Have you ever thought about it?' asked Neha.

One of her roommates responded, 'I think she is right. Would I consider working here next year? Yes, I would. Free boarding and lodging and a salary that could increase with yearly increments. So, other than work pressure what other factors could force me to leave? Something out of the ordinary...' her voice trailed off when her attempts to find a credible explanation reached a dead end.

Another roommate firmly stated, 'We just need to be more vigilant. Observe everything very closely from now on. If we go out, we should do it in groups and never alone.'

Neha secretly vowed to take a pocket knife with her on such trips. When they heard the shower tap close, they exchanged glances to warn each other that the new inmate would be out any minute and pretended to busy themselves with school work.

Prem's disappointment of being unemployed on being conferred Master of Business Administration degree ended with his appointment at Paramesh Technofab, New Delhi. The employment opportunity also ended the weekend travel to Coimbatore. Weekends became tedious and to relieve themselves of boredom, those staff who chose to stay, commenced their trips to the local park. The presence of a group of well dressed, attractive, young women chatting and laughing, throwing caution to wind did not go unnoticed by youthful male opportunists.

When Neha and her friends exited the park before darkness descended on the town, the opportunists convinced themselves that it was their moral responsibility to escort the women to their haven in their silver-grey fiat. It was only when the fiat circumnavigated them for the third time did the damsels realise that they were in distress. Neha was quick to spot the writing on the top right hand corner of the fiat's tinted rear glass in white stylistic font that read 'Varun'. Giddiness, excitement and apprehension mirrored on the young ladies' animated features. Their quickened pace decelerated only when they had reached the safety of the school compound.

That excursion to the park was followed by many more jaunts and the ladies never returned disappointed as they were always escorted by the fiat. Even Neha looked forward to spotting the fiat on their outings as she did not regard temporary digressions sinful. Then approached the inauspicious day when Fate rolled the dice and Deception danced stealthily in the dead of the night. Neha, who had devoured more than the usual servings of kichadi due to its irresistible palatableness, slept like a log as soon as she crept into her bed.

Voices were muffled, strong hands lifted Neha's feminine physique, carried her comatose figure gingerly down the flight of steps into the backseat of a van with a noiseless engine and was driven to an undivulged locale concealed by the waterfalls. Celestial bodies witnessed the disrobing of human dignity in abomination while the moonlight caressed away the vestige of perverse mauling that was captured on celluloid after which she was returned.

Anonymous conspirators within the establishment had facilitated and superintended that night's covert exploitation.

Neha woke up feeling invaded to a dazzling day completely clueless about the previous night's nefariousness. Unable to decipher the cause for her current emotional state, she cruised through the day's routines unshaken and unmoved.

THREE

HURDLES

Neha busied herself with weekdays' morning routines as usual wondering what the outcome of the interview would be. She had requested Sarah, the Teacher's Federation Women's contact officer to be present at the meeting and support her through the process. Sarah had readily consented although she was flabbergasted at the turn of events. Before she left for school, she ensured that the counter response she had spent some time formulating, was in her bag as she intended to give it to the DP before the meeting commenced. She consoled herself that she would emerge unscathed from that hurdle just as every other stumbling block she had jumped over.

Within a fortnight, since her migration to Australia, Neha's waters broke due to an unanticipated loss of balance and tumble in a shared accommodation bathtub when she was heavily pregnant. The waters incessant flow could not be interrupted for hours. Like a broken dam, everything on her and in the vicinity, was completely drenched augmenting the chilliness that was creeping into second floor unit as Autumn bade farewell to the encroaching Winter. It being the first pregnancy, Neha spent that night of May 2003 agonising about complications associated with the breaking of waters, regretting the late-night showering decision and shivering in the dampness in which she was submerged. That catastrophic night was followed by hospitalisation the next day and as there were no signs of contractions, after a 48-hour wait induced labour became inevitable.

Little did Neha know that the procedure would be excruciatingly painful. The Nitrous oxide inhaled via a mouthpiece, which relieved her from pain temporarily, assaulted her with double the force when the effects of the gas wore off. The walls of the labour room resonated Neha's screams of frustration and groans of pain. After several hours of futile gas inhaling, Neha's relentless pain was eventually numbed with the administration of Epidural. Amidst chorused "push" and patterned breathing Neha painlessly pushed out a healthy baby boy, crossing the barrier of childbirth exultantly.

Three months later, when things and friends fell apart; when shared accommodation ceased being shared; Neha and Prem with their baby John moved from Fourth Avenue, Campsie to a $150 per week two-bedroom unit with shared laundry on Gould Street, Campsie. The nuclear family failed to foresee the dangers of inhabiting a century-old building that showed signs of deterioration and contained sections that required repair. Neha recalled how within few weeks of shifting into the new unit they had befriended a few Indian couples, with and without children, who invited them to dinners, festivities and celebrations and vice versa.

With the advent of 2004 Chinese New Year, contentment experienced by the bourgeois family suffered a temporary setback. None of the families in the six units of that building predicted the existence of a threat in the shared laundry on that fateful night. Even when Prem returned from DKP knitting factory, Alexandria, after his shift at 8:00 pm that crucial evening, did Neha suspect that something destructive and uncontrollably wild was raging within the four walls of that shared space. Dinner was prepared and laid out on the dining table donated by St. Vincent de Paul's Society. Neha was astute enough to check the quality of furniture at Vinnies before choosing between exhausting their limited savings on new ones and relying on good quality charitable donations. She decided in favour of the latter.

Deep slumber claimed their exhausted bodies the moment they reclined on their inviting beds. Neha woke up startled by the loud banging on the door. Or so she imagined. However, when she turned to wake her snoring better-half, she was dazzled to see multi-coloured lights flashing through the blinds of the bedroom window.

Prem's mumble, 'I think you're hallucinating. Since the birth of John, you have been showing signs of insomnia,' forced Neha out of her bed to satisfy her curiosity.

She was aghast as she was not prepared for the sight below.

'Prem, wake up. I'm serious. You're not going to believe this,' said Neha noticing two fire trucks, an ambulance and few police cars lined just outside the building.

Neha's powerful shriek, when she realised that one of the fire truck's hose was passing through the entrance of the ground floor of their building, roused Prem to wakefulness. The distinct banging grew louder and louder in their ears. Prem reached the bedroom door in two long strides and when he opened it the smoke-filled, char-odoured, heat-generating hall, paralysed him into immobility. Through the hazy vision, he saw the silhouettes of bulky firefighters.

On approaching him, one of the firefighters ducked him forcefully instructing him, 'Stay that way until you walk out of the door'.

Prem allowed himself to be escorted by another rescuer through the singed door-less threshold to the kerbside, where the pyjama-clad occupants of other units had gathered in stunned silence while repeatedly reminding the firefighters, 'My wife and my baby are in the bedroom.'

Neha's attempts to lower the blanket-wrapped baby through the bedroom window with tied bedsheets were cut short by the firefighters, who ushered her with her head ducked under the smoke clouds, to the kerbside, where Prem awaited her arrival anxiously. The drowsy fire victims tolerated an indefinite wait until the rescuers extinguished the fire, severed electricity connection, investigated what triggered the fire and re-assessed safety factors. The mystery of the anonymous caller was solved when the fire fighters revealed that a tenant in the building behind theirs, who was shocked to discover the laundry ablaze at midnight, had placed the call for help. An old electric clothes dryer that had malfunctioned was the catalyst for the fire that spread to the units on either side of the shared laundry after having silently devoured it.

The occupants, who thanked the stars and their fortune for having survived death and fatal burn injuries, witnessed the birth of the Chinese New Year from the kerbside. It was almost dawn when they gained access to their fire ravaged units and almost noon when electricity connection was restored. Although the accident was life-threatening, it did not have devastating consequences on the residents as the fire was controlled from spreading beyond the doors of the units.

Economically, Neha reflected, things were not always on the bright side even though they made ends meet. She recalled how a consultation with Pediatric Surgeon Dr. Young revealed that two months old John's sleeplessness and incessant wailing was due to hernia, which had to be surgically removed. If Neha wanted Dr. Young to perform the surgery she would have to bear the expenses, which was unaffordable at that period as they were still newly arrived migrants without permanent employment and handsome income. She was confronted with a tough decision. She was compelled to choose between an expensive, experienced surgeon with no records of failure or post-operative complications and junior doctors in training, who would charge only the no gap fee. She did not hesitate to discuss her precarious predicament with Dr. Young who asked her, 'How long have you been in the country?'

'Hardly three months,' replied Neha.

'Hmm… and none of you are employed?' questioned Dr. Young.

Prem said, 'I am working as a room attendant. I must make do with this job until I find a position suitable for my qualifications. My income is adequate only to pay the rent, groceries etc.'

The surgeon was silent for a few seconds before stating, 'in that case I recommend the junior doctor option. Let's proceed with the date for the surgery.'

On the day of the surgery, Neha and Prem whiled away two long hours with purposeless, light-hearted banter to conceal the grimness of the situation until they were interrupted by one of the hospital nurses who said, 'Baby John is in his bed. You can see him now.'

They were relieved to find John in his bed heavily drugged as the effects of intravenously administered monitored anaesthesia was yet to wear off.

Dr. Young walked towards them flashing a broad smile and said,

'The surgery is a success. You have nothing to worry about as the junior doctors performed the operation under my supervision.'

Neha wasted no time in expressing her gratitude, 'Thank you. You do not know how much this means to me.'

Nodding his head in acknowledgement, he added, 'If there are no concerns John would be discharged in an hour or two without much ado.'

As Neha was rustling through the pages of memory, realisation dawned on her that most migrants encounter barricades, which they tussle to overcome. The land of opportunities that appeared greener when they were on the other side of the world deceptively veiled the harsh terrains, which could only be transformed into fertile oasis with the passage of time and tough grind. Like thousands of migrants, who on their arrival, pursue the Great Australian Dream of home ownership, stable work and comfortable retirement, Neha gaining a tertiary qualification from an Australian university became a state school employee and owned a three-bedroom home in a cul-de-sac in the suburb of Ingleburn. She thought that if she could conquer the initial impediments with determined purpose she had no qualms about facing an interview on hostile grounds.

Neha was summoned to the conference room during period 2 and as she dragged the chair to perch, she saw few familiar faces that wielded authority and a few that were belligerent. The gruelling attack mode was activated with the victim deprived of any chance to defend herself. Every attempt to mend her ruined reputation was to no avail with the right to freedom of speech denied. Neha's efforts to refute the accusations or utterances to clarify were stonewalled several times. She was on the brink of bellowing due to emotional imbalance when the DP for Year 11 and 12, Mr. Declan, lowered his voice and gestured to step outside the interrogation room. The timely distraction served to hold her flaring temper in check and made her receptive to the friendly advice offered.

'Please don't take this any other way. I'm not saying that you are entirely at fault. I think we both know that they're trying to provoke you,' whispered Mr. Declan.

Neha could not stop herself from remarking, 'They are not fair. They are piling accusations and do not allow me to speak. Every time I try to say something in my defense they talk over me.'

'Like I said, they are trying to provoke you into raising your voice so that they can enforce the Code of Conduct. I'm your well-wisher. Take my advice and apologize to the complainant. Just say that you won't repeat it again. That way they will have to conclude the meeting,' pointed out Mr. Declan.

Her options being limited, Neha preferred the wise enemy rather than the foolish friend.

Weighing her chances of success, Neha responded, 'Okay.'

Her return was greeted with hushed conversations. The insincere remorse Neha flung at her assailants resulted in stupefaction. The defeatists, vanquished in their ulterior motive, sat in awkward silence with priceless grimaces of disappointment on their unhappy countenances. The interrogation was concluded, authorities dismissed, agreement finalised, signatured and filed only to be dispatched to oblivion.

The omniscient deity intervened and turned the wheel of fortune by removing the perpetrators mysteriously from the establishment with prospects of overseas employment and transfer with promotions. The environment became conducive once again for Neha, who preferred to remain standoffish, a strategy that shielded her from cunning manipulators and character assassins. The revelation that she would always be a second-class citizen to a biased community that failed to value the contributions of a racially diverse educator despite the efforts invested, immersed her in existential angst. Branded volatile and boisterous, alienated by individuals with vested interests, misplaced, mistreated and misunderstood, Neha cruised through a period of hibernation.

Additional responsibilities offered to heal the etched scars were more like a snare intended for failure. In varied roles of leadership, Neha strictly adhered to professionalism and though staff members underestimated her prowess, tested her or exchanged glances over a mispronounced word, Neha discounted the hitches each time only to surface victoriously. Retrospectively, she surmised that the unavailability of willing staff to shoulder such responsibilities was what made her the preferred option. At the completion of the office, a reluctant recognition or sparing acknowledgement was doled as it was customary or tradition. Or so she reasoned.

The course of a non-conformist never did run smooth. Exclusion, isolation and collective sabotage characterised Neha's life at her workplace. Occasionally, hostility raged with stirred students hurling racial slurs, books and objects at her; with staff and students directing callous comments and indifferent looks towards her with the dishonourable intention of incapacitating her from work. Irrespective of the incitement, the divide and rule policy did not have the desired effect on her as she continued to excel in leadership opportunities provided by external agencies. Adamantly, she persevered in the conviction that knowledge, which is limitless, needed to be imparted to an intolerant community that attached excessive significance to trade and failed to see formal education as a means of social upliftment. Thick-skinned, unruffled and nameless she voyaged through stormy seas and calamitous currents.

FOUR

PURLOINED

Neha's heart raced when she noticed the lit hall through the window as she halted her car in the driveway. She desperately wished for her suspicions to be untrue as she had very distinct memory of not having turned the lights on before heading for work. The rooms were flooded with ample sunlight in the mornings that the expediency of switching on the electrical lights was unreal. The practice of leaving lights on after the deed was done could mean only one thing, as this was not the first-time she had intruders while she was away. She stumbled out of the car and stepped into the garden below her window to scan the room through the partially opened blinds for missing objects and her heart sank when she discovered the vacant, dustless area on the TV furniture which used to be occupied by John's Nintendo console. The drawers of the TV stand left open confirmed that the games were burgled too. Through the doorway of the hall, she could see the well-lit corridor and decided against entering the house as she did not fancy becoming a prey to lurking predators.

Neha told John, whose face was contorted with fear, 'Stay in the car. Call your dad and tell him about the break in.'

On the completion of formalities such as contacting the police and the real estate agent, who assured that the owner of the property would join her in a short while, Neha rested her aching legs by sinking in to the driver's seat. She left the vehicle's door open to relieve herself from the suffocation that was overwhelming her. The thievery rendered her new rented accommodation unsafe to live. It was time to move as she had been the target a second time within a gap of two months. Six months ago, she was living in a jointly owned independent house, however, a change of circumstances had eventuated her tenancy at her current residence.

As a car horn sounded, John scrambled out of the car and muttered a hasty, 'Goodbye mum. Be safe!'

Her gaze followed him fondly until he disappeared into Prem's car. As she watched the back of the car disappear into an alleyway adjacent to the property, a candid consciousness that she would be solitary in times of such misfortune could not be dismissed. An hour's wait made her irate as the cops had not arrived at the crime scene and when questioned, their response that they had other cases that required immediate attention, was of no consolation. Neha was waiting in the car sleepy-eyed when the property owner and his wife, who were working in the local bank, made an appearance.

Together they toured the property only to discover the shattered glass of the window and the wrenched fly screen in the dining room, through which the electronic-goods-stealers gained access into the property. Patterned thievery through windows of the property were on the rise in the neighbourhood of Ingleburn and Glenfield. The first rushed break-in materialized through the deliberately tampered window of the first bedroom and only the electronics goods at first notice were stolen. But for the content insurance, the second larceny would have been a drain on her purse, Neha thought, as she surveyed the growing list of stolen items that she was most likely to locate within a few days in pawn shops or at Cash Converters. The Indonesian owners, who joined her in the fruitless wait for the police, departed leaving her safety in the hands of the almighty. Neha's decision to spend the night alone in the house with a man-made portal, instead of considering alternate arrangements, was regarded by the couple as a choice lacking wisdom.

The anticipated boys in blue eventually arrived, breezed through the property and informed her that a cop from the forensic department would arrive at the appointed hour to scan the property for fingerprints and other clues that could lead to the criminals. When in solitude, Neha removed the heavy books from a bookshelf, before she moved it from its original spot to block the open space created by the larcenists. She knew that the bookshelf was an ineffective barrier for a determined intruder, however, the noise created by dislodged books, if the bookshelf was disturbed, would awaken her from an unconscious state. She would then have time to dash to the garage, lock the connecting door which separated the house from the garage and remain concealed in the car. Her sharpened senses made it impossible for her to bat an eyelid throughout the night as she was conscious of every little sound and movement.

Fatigued mind strayed into the foyers of nostalgia. Separate lives seemed to be the only sensible solution as Prem and Neha were mentally and emotionally so distant that they barely recognised each other and what they had meant to each other. Was it the liberated Australian culture that erected an indestructible wall between them? Or was it the societal sexual opportunism that terminated a long-standing relationship that was built on the foundations of trust and fidelity? That pivotal day, which concluded the hate-love relationship with no possibility of a reunion, was clearly etched in her memory.

'I will be going to Curves now and will be back in an hour,' Neha said to Prem, who was heavily intoxicated as he had moved on to the second bottle of scotch during TV viewing with the volume being deafeningly loud.

His tendency to indulge in unnecessary, insensible bickering made her impatient and explosive and that evening one such heated exchange had just ended with six-year-old John bearing the brunt of it for taking his mother's side. A hard slap on his chubby little cheek had left a red imprint that took several minutes to fade. Neha perceived the manoeuvre as a father's response to a sign of disrespect rather than of any concern, even though she was furious. Not only was she pressured into applying for a divorce for a reason that she was unaware of other than incompatibility, but she was swindled out of spouse settlement and child support. The promise of sole ownership of the jointly owned house remained unfulfilled, the arrival of a piece of paper that legally terminated marital relationship from Paramatta magistrate established the fact that living under the same roof as partners was unlawful and having to tolerate Prem's drunken abusive behaviour on a regular basis pushed Neha over the edge.

'John, stay on the sofa and watch TV until mum returns. Don't argue with your Dad.'

'Yes Mamma.'

'Don't go', said Prem.

'Why should I listen to you? You're officially my ex-husband now. Every time I try to knock myself into shape and you start to notice the difference you cause unnecessary problems. I am out of here.'

Neha slammed the front door shut and drove out of the cul-de-sac like a bat out of hell with screeching tyres, into the main road. Thirty minutes on the Curves circuit was followed by stretch exercises and it was rejuvenating for Neha to feel the beads of perspiration break into trickles of sweat down her body. The workout session had a calming effect on her emotionally high strung personality. Feeling relaxed and contended she drove home, parked the car in the driveway and not having an inkling of what lay in store, she opened the front door with her keys.

'Hey John, I am back,' Neha called out as she stepped into the hall.

Something about the uncanny frozen expression on his face spoke volumes to her. She gingerly balanced herself on the sofa next to him, put her arms around his shoulders and gazed into his tear stained face for few seconds before she posed the question, 'What happened?'

He shook his head spasmodically in disagreement as if the Damocles sword hanging over his head would slice him into two if he revealed the dark, hidden facts.

'John, if you're scared to tell me I can take you to the cops.'

After a moment of indeterminacy, he sprang up with hope bringing a sparkle to his stunned, dejected face. The fact that he consented to confide in a cop not only immersed Neha in disbelief but also emphasised the grimness of what had ensued in her absence. It was not until they had exited the house and reached the safety of the car did John disclose to Neha that he was chased around the house, slapped and hit twenty times by his inebriated parent. Although she was dubious about the accuracy of the number provided, there was no denying that it was a case of abuse and she was in consensus with her six-year-old son who yearned for the law to intervene, to chastise an irresponsible adult who had inflicted pain and humiliation.

Neha parked the car in front of Macquarie Fields Police Station and heaved a sigh of relief when brave John stepped out of the car and strode confidently through the glass doors to the information desk. Neha quickly briefed them about the unfortunate turn of events, which was followed by an elucidation of the interview procedures.

Officer Simpson stated, 'How this works is that the victim will be interviewed by two Police officers. John will be taken to a room with audio visual recording equipment. Meet Officer Kate Byrnes and Officer Ferguson.'

Neha greeted them with a terse, 'Hello' which was matched by an equally concise chorused, 'Hi there!'

Officer Simpson continued, "They will be interviewing John once the formalities are over. The interview would be recorded and filmed, burned on a DVD to be played in court."

Neha distractedly replied, 'I understand,' as she could hear the hearty laughter of the officers who were preparing John for the interview by striking amiable conversations with him.

John was whisked away for a half-an-hour interview while Neha amused herself with the posters and other visuals displayed in the police station, besides the few expressionless and lost individuals who accessed the wending machine.

John believed in vain that sanity would be restored in his little, fun-filled orderly world as poetic justice prevailed.

Neha's observations were cut short when Officer Simpson declared, 'We will come out to your place to warn your husband that he is not to touch you or John until he leaves. He will be given two or three hours to pack the essential items and arrange an alternate accommodation. It will take an hour or two to get the ADVO ready. Once the paper work is ready we will escort him out of the property and he is not to come within 100 metres of your property.'

The magnitude of the mess was not fully comprehended by Prem as his alcohol laced brain impaired his reasoning, words uttered to him were mere sounds which failed to register and Neha's forewarning about the forthcoming events fell on muffled, malfunctioning ears.

It was 8'0 clock when the police arrived, camouflaged in the darkness, which had established its supremacy over the orange black sunset skies. The officers minced matters, emphasised the mandatory requirements of ADVO and departed instructing the alcoholic to pack his things as change of residence was inevitable under the circumstances. Perplexed and astounded that people who were once dear to him had become strangers and had resorted to law, Prem struggled to remember the day's occurrences and to come to terms with reality. Overwhelmed by alcohol induced exhaustion he drifted into a coma, which shut him out from his self-initiated abusive world for a few hours, oblivious of the police's return with paperwork.

'Wake up. Wake up,' repeated Officer Simpson in ascending tone to Prem who had succumbed to the solace of deep sleep on the carpet in the middle of the living room.

A few taps and shakes brought Prem to a wakeful state, who bewildered, attempted in vain to encipher the reason behind the unexpected disturbance by the law enforcers.

'We have an AVO in your name. You need to pack a few

emergency things to help you through the night like phone, wallet, change of clothes etc. and come with us.'

'What?' 'Why?' was all Neha heard Prem vocalise as he struggled to stand without assistance from his sitting posture. His speech was not slurred as intoxication had worn off and erased any memory of the day's disastrous developments that would have otherwise clung to his normally functioning temporal lobes.

'A complain was lodged by your son and wife this evening. We made it very clear when we arrived earlier that you should be packed and ready to leave,' explained Officer Simpson with a second police officer playing the role of a passive bystander.

'I don't remember. I don't remember anything. What have I done? Why are you arresting me?' stated Prem whose voice cracked with emotion.

Tears trickled down his eyes and for a second Neha felt her heart in her throat and everything come to a standstill. Pain and suffocation strangled her as she had involuntarily become a judge who had issued a death sentence to an innocent man. Tables turned and Neha came across as a cold, heartless, heinous bitch, who rendered a man homeless for unknown selfish reasons. Even the officers could not help but sympathise with him as he was clueless like an amnesia affected person.

John was asleep in his room. The officers had deliberately timed their late arrival to spare the child the guilt and the burden of having to witness his father being escorted by the police.

Neha contemplated withdrawing the complaint when she saw Prem sobbing like a child while reiterating, 'I have nowhere to go. This is my house. I have no one. I never thought she would do this to me.'

'Come with us. We will find you a place. Just take a few necessary things for the night. You can send someone tomorrow to get the rest,' comforted Officer Simpson.

Bawling his eyes out, he searched for his phone, wallet, keys and a few other things through hazy vision. Neha stood paralysed watching the tragic, melancholic scene unfold before her tearless eyes, and in that crucial moment she was in accordance with Shakespeare's truthful observation, *"As flies to wanton boys, are we to the gods; they kill us for their sport"*. A part of her was immune to pain, numbed by humiliating experiences and hatred while the part that had known finer emotions, powerless to alter the course of events, chose to remain nonchalant.

When the first rays of dawn filtered through the bedroom window, Neha noticed that her unplanned visit down the memory lane had accelerated time and when sleep claimed heavy eyelids she did not resist.

FIVE

VOICES FROM THE PAST

'A nother day, another dollar,' Neha heard Mr. Gary, the Head Teacher of Administration call out to a newly appointed casual.

She congratulated herself on her decision to validate her academic credentials from overseas by obtaining a tertiary qualification. She was fortunate to be in a substantive position for more than 9 years in a state school. At least she did not have to worry about day to day employment or blocks anymore. As she was in a hurry to reach her classroom on the first floor, she did not think it worthwhile to cast a backward glance to satisfy her curiosity about who the new casual staff was. There would always be a time for that as the school would find ways to provide temporary arrangements to casual teachers as they were in demand.

The mornings were usually busy commencing with 20 minutes' roll call followed by two sixty minutes' periods. Neha was relieved to hear the bell as she was not having an easy day with one of her classes displaying challenging patterns of behaviour. How she longed for a cup of coffee!!

Neha made her way to the English staff room reflecting on how all her attempts to manage classroom behaviour by implementing the school's discipline policies were dashed to the ground. Students were becoming less academically oriented each day and her attempts to sustain interest in the current topic by integrating technology based lessons were not successful to the extent she had imagined.

When she opened the door to the common room and was making her way blindly to the English staff room she heard a female voice cry out in astonishment, 'Oh my God! Is that you?'

Neha turned around and came face to face with an attractive looking woman, whom she recognized immediately as she did not look very different from when she was a school student. She could not believe her eyes as she was staring at Rachel, who was her classmate in Fifth Standard. They were schooled at one of the reputed catholic institutions in Coimbatore, where they grew up.

Neha struggled to overcome her surprise and all she could blurt out was, 'the world is a small place after all.'

Her chances of meeting a schoolmate three decades later in another country working in the same educational institution would have been remote and would have sounded incredible till that moment.

Within the remaining twenty-five minutes of recess, they had managed to bridge a gap of thirty-five years by filling in the unknown details of each other's lives.

'I came to Australia in 2003 in my advanced stages of pregnancy with my partner. When did you arrive?' asked Neha.

'Two years ago,' replied Rachel.

'Are you here as a day-to-day casual or on a temporary block?'

'Day-to-day. Being a mother of two, this arrangement suits me. My hubby is in a permanent position. He is the Bank Manager at Sunpac, Macarthur Square. We're able to manage.'

'How old are the children'?

'My daughter is thirteen and son is five years old. How old is your child?'

Neha replied, 'My boy is twelve years old. I am single now. I went through an unpleasant divorce a few years ago. I knew that you went back to your parents, who were employed in the middle east when you were in the Sixth Standard. What did you do after you left Coimbatore?'

'I finished my schooling abroad. I completed my Bachelor degree in Kerala and then got married.'

The ear-piercing shriek of the school bell ended the exhilarating drivel between the two estranged friends and Neha found herself hurrying to the print room to collect student worksheets for period 4. Rachel had to head back to her tentative classes allocated for the day.

'Strange! Of all the places at Wakefield. Even worse I cannot stop smiling,' thought Neha to herself.

She had to deliberately counterfeit a grim facade as she walked through the creaking wooden corridors of the institution, which seemed to share her elated emotion. Neha hastily retrieved the worksheets from her pigeon hole and retraced her path down the same corridor as the desire for a refreshing cup of coffee urged her to keep walking until she reached the staff room.

'Finally,' said Neha to herself and as she prepared her coffee, the tantalising aroma reanimated her and coerced her to plop in her chair.

As Neha was sipping her beverage, memory lane chose to walk her through a day so heinous when Rachel and she encountered their worst nightmares while returning from school.

* * * *

It was 31ˢᵗ October 1984. A day no different than any other and Neha, who was then ten years old was making some final touches to her crease-less white shirt tucked into a pleated blue skirt that reached to her knees and double knotted polyester blue tie with the school emblem embroidered on it. Little did she know what the day had in store for her or for the nation. Her neighbourhood friend Shiela, who was waiting outside her house, was reminding her for the second time that they were running late and would have to face the wrath of Sr. Patricia, who made it her mission to chastise latecomers.

Neha sprinted with Shiela down the street to the main road as it took a good thirty minutes' walk along Saibaba Colony Road to the school and if they did not make it to the assembly when the first bell rang all hell would be let loose. They were fortunate to avoid detection and merged in to the serpentine lines into which students arranged themselves for the assembly. Principal's loud greeting over the microphone, few quick announcements by student leaders and few reminders about the consequences that would be meted out if rules were violated saw the end of the assembly.

As Neha and Shiela belonged to different class divisions, they nodded to each other and headed to their respective classes. Half way through the lesson the bell rang continuously for two minutes, which was unusual, and the teachers asked students to head to the quad for an emergency assembly.

'I just received a call from the Commissioner of Police. Our Prime Minister Indira Gandhi has been shot and her condition is critical...' announced the Principal, who was on the brink of bursting in to tears, which evoked a loud collective gasp of disbelief from students who could not comprehend how someone so powerful with Z security could be shot.

Students' attempts to initiate conversations were quickly subdued as the Principal continued that they would have to leave for their homes immediately, as parts of the district had already witnessed political upheaval.

'Group disperse.'

Students scattered in different directions hoping that the Prime Minister would survive, and Neha tried to find Shiela amidst a thousand students heading for the main gates of the school.

'The gates. That's it!' Neha remarked to herself.

She waited outside the gates and caught Shiela, who was frantically searching for her with worry written all over her face. Neha waved to Shiela and relief washed over her downcast face.

She even managed a smile while saying, 'We need to reach home before things happen.'

Once they hit the main road they slowed down their pace and began to arrive at their own conclusions on who could have committed such a nefarious crime. They would have surpassed the CID/CIA in deciphering the motif behind the assassination attempt, if they had not been interrupted by a commotion a few meters away from where they were.

The girls were forced to linger as political activists wearing white shirts and khakhi pants belonging to the Rashtriya Swayamsevak Sang were verbally abusing a few catholic school students, who were mistaken to be Sikh girls as they shared the phenotype of Punjabis. Few RSS workers grabbed school bags of students, whom they suspected to be Sikhs and checked the names on their exercise books to confirm if they were being truthful about their origin while screaming out things like, 'Teach the Sikhs a lesson!'

It was not hard to construe that the riots were triggered by the murder attempt on the Prime Minister and a passionate outcry, 'If it were not for the Sikh bodyguards the PM would have been alive. You bastards have killed madam. Seek blood for blood!' spelled out to Neha and the crowd why the RSS workers had turned unanticipatedly anti-Sikh.

Pedestrians, who were of a darker complexion or had the appearance or features of a typical South Indian, were allowed to pass without much ado. Shiela turned to the left and noticed Rachel and another friend of theirs Komal Sunda hop off their bicycles in confusion, wondering about the cause for the unexpected interception.

Shiela turned to me and whispered, 'I don't know what is going to happen to Komal.'

When the magnitude of what Shiela was implying dawned on Neha she waded through the crowd and reached Komal and Rachel.

She had to act quickly and in less than a minute she explained to Komal, 'The RSS workers were abusive to some students who looked like Punjabis. They were also checking school bags.'

Komal stared at Neha with widened eyes and asked, 'What am I going to do now?'

'Let's exchange our bags. Try not to look so worried,' said Neha to Komal and Rachel, who were wondering if the plan would work.

They decided to stick together and when it was their turn the RSS worker allowed Neha, Sheila and Rachel to pass through without the slightest reluctance but stopped Komal just as they had anticipated.

Upon interrogation, Komal turned out to be a wicked little actress, who lied that her name was Neha with such confidence and handed the school bag to the RSS worker in a matter of fact manner, that for a second even Neha doubted if the name belonged to her. Much to the girls' relief the activist checked the name on her exercise book and allowed her to pass through. They rushed from the spot like bats out of hell and broke the awkward silence only when they were hundred meters away from the scene that petrified the living daylights out of them. Rachel and Komal jumped on to their bicycles, waved their goodbyes and turned into the Post and Telegraph quarters where they resided, while Neha and Shiela continued to walk until they reached their neighbourhood.

1984 was also the year which saw the advent of colour television in Coimbatore, the textile and engineering city of India. Neha's father, Vincent, prided himself on his decision to have purchased one. National telecasts commenced in 1982 via the only national channel, Doordarshan and at a time when the entire nation was drowned in sorrow over the death of the first woman Prime Minister of India, the colour television gained a unique significance, with the possibility of information world unfolding right before the viewers in their own dwellings being definite. Vincent arrived home exasperated an hour after Neha and vocalising how the acquisition of colour television was timely, switched it on, ordering his wife Stella to bring him a cup of tea.

Vincent enquired Neha about the occurrences at school and as usual she provided him with an elaborate description of every minute detail with the conversation culminating in a brief explanation. Vincent elucidated how the late PM's efforts to suppress a group of extremists, who were living in The Golden Temple in Punjab, with an iron hand by carrying out Operation Blue Star resulted in her brutal murder, which was executed by her Sikh bodyguards that day.

* * * *

Once again, her journey into the past was cut short unceremoniously by the school bell which brought her to the present world abruptly. She looked around her in confusion to ascertain her whereabouts. She realised that she was still in the staffroom and period 4 had just commenced. It was expedient for her to be present in the classroom when students arrived as any deviation from usual routines resulted in pandemonium.

'Rachel can wait. There will be a time to renew the disconnected bonds of friendship,' Neha thought to herself as she bolted up the stairs to outdistance her students.

She had to remind herself that renewing ties was not exactly her forte. Most acquaintances would describe her as elusive and she preferred to stay that way.

SIX

SHADOWS

More than an hour's wait at Sydney International Airport coerced Neha into sojourns of nostalgia. Despite the arrival of Singapore Airlines at the expected time there were no signs of passengers at the entrance of Gate 59. It took ten years for this anticipated reunion with her estranged family and it did not come without a price. A divorce. Neha, who was regarded as the black sheep of the family, for choosing a life partner from another caste had to be punished with ostracism.

Her fourteen-year-old son's query about what was causing the delay interrupted her train of thought. She dragged herself from her journey into yesteryear and tried to think of a convincing reply to silence him for some time. After explaining to him briefly about security concerns and the lengthy wait passengers usually had to tolerate to collect their bags, Neha distracted herself with a news item published in The Sydney Morning Herald that she was clutching in her left hand. *"Boost to Turnbull as Coalition takes the lead in two more cliffhanger seats"* held her interest long enough to continue scanning the first few lines of the report, *"The Coalition has won a key cliffhanger seat and leads in two more, boosting Malcolm Turnbull's chances of forming a majority government...."* when a sudden shriek from her excited son John, 'They are coming!' startled her in to dropping the newspaper.

Neha turned sharply to the entrance of the gate, where an ocean of passengers flooded down the ramp, only to scatter in different directions like ants responding to the slightest disturbance. Her eyes searched for familiarity in the sea of exhausted, jet-lagged and curiously contented passengers until her vision registered on the sparkling visage of her brother, George. He was excitedly chatting to his two-year-old daughter Anne and his wife Mona, whose beaming smile was infectious even in that fleeting glimpse. Her incessant search continued until her gaze collided with a pair of anxious eyes with tears glistening in them, threatening to run down her pale plump cheeks that has begun to show signs of decrepitude. She breathed a sigh of relief and held the emotional turbulence that welled up within her in check. She waited patiently for them to reach within proximity to initiate any amiable greeting or conversation.

'How are you mum? You must be feeling exhausted after the long journey,' said Neha embracing her.

'I think I survived my first flight journey. How have you been? Can't believe that I had to wait this long to see you,' exclaimed Stella in a shaky voice encircling her arms around Neha bringing her even closer to her.

Neha smiled at her sister-in-law Mona, who was just a name, a face on Facebook and a voice over the phone till that eventful day. She could not recall clearly if she had been invited or just informed of her brother's wedding. At the end of the lengthy telephone conversation with mum, Dad and George she could not dismiss the feeling that she was not expected to attend. The present was more important than the past reasoned Neha.

'I am glad to see you. I have been looking forward to this visit,' said Neha giving her a quick hug.

'Me too,' replied Mona.

She added to her two-year-old daughter Anne who was engrossed in conversation with John, 'Are you happy to see Neha Aunty?'

'Yes, I am. I am happy to see John too,' she remarked enthusiastically.

A few minutes after the initial excited greetings, they found themselves journeying in a maxi cab with a contended expression on their fatigued countenances as the moment held promise of forthcoming days of bliss and catch-up prattle that usually follows a family reunion. Neha threw a furtive glance at her mother, who was still struggling to regain her composure, and yet she felt that there was a part of her that could not be reached. She had been like that ever since that fatal day, which not only transformed her life for ever, but also the lives of those around her significantly. Neha did not have to rustle through the pages of childhood memories in India as vivid details of that catastrophic day flooded to her mind effortlessly.

* * *

'She is not in her room. I searched for her everywhere. Where could she have gone in the wee small hours of the morning?'

Neha was not sure if she was labouring under some illusion or if she was wading through a nightmare, which was suffocating her and pulling her deep into it like a bog mire, and yet the voices seemed so real.

'What was happening? Why was my mother not in her room? Why was someone calling my name out loud?' she wondered.

She felt someone shake her vehemently and when she succeeded in the arduous task of opening her eyes, she struggled to focus in the dimly lit room trying to comprehend what was causing all the commotion around her at midnight. Her eyes swam through the room until it locked on the face of her aunt who looked pale. Angst had aged her within the span of an evening or so it seemed to her.

'Stella is not in her room. I looked for her everywhere in the house. I did not suspect anything as we were all in a festive mood and the celebrations of St. Antony's feast had kept us up all night. Your father is looking for her in the neighbourhood,' finished Aunt in a rush.

Neha sat up in her bed shocked and bewildered until the full impact of the revelation sank on her. She ran in and out of all the rooms searching for her missing mother and wishing desperately that it was all a horrible mistake and that her mother was somewhere in the house. As an answer to her prayers, Neha heard her mother's voice followed by her father's, which betrayed his herculean efforts to hold his temper in check while trying to discover the reason for her unexplained flight at midnight, defaming him and opening avenues for unwanted gossip and scandal.

Stella's dishevelled appearance and dark circles under her sleepless pale dead fish eyes had a different tale to tell. Her attempts to explain why she fled from the house left the entire family dumbfounded and speechless. Neha stood there paralysed when she heard her mother say that if she had not left the house her aunties would have murdered her. Neha turned to Aunt Rosie and Aunt

Lucy only to see shock engraved on their faces as though they were encountering their worst nemesis.

Neha heard her father respond to one of her uncles' questions, '... I found her at Matthew's house, who is a very good friend of ours. His older son, who was at the gates of the house, called out to me when he saw me walking down the street. I was relieved to hear that Stella was at their place. They were trying to calm her down as she was hysterical.'

Uncle Anthony, who was married to Aunt Rosie and an epitome of patience, advised Vincent, Neha's father, to comfort Stella rather than accuse her and to contact her father about the strange occurrences. To Neha's consternation, he added that they would like to leave in the morning under the circumstances. Neha's heart reached out to her father who was perplexed, humiliated and was unsure of what course of action he had to take. However, he followed Uncle Anthony's advice and even though the rest of the family tried to drown their sorrows in the solace of slumber, most of them failed to succeed.

Things did not improve the next morning when Stella's father arrived. He squashed every attempt of Neha's aunts to turn the unfortunate event around, and who despite his exhaustion from the eight hours unplanned journey during the night, preferred the path of accusation. Vincent's efforts to stop his sisters from leaving proved futile and Stella left with her father for Chennai. Neha ran to embrace Vincent, who looked devastated and vulnerable, to relieve him from the trauma that was choking him and forcing him to withdraw into a place inside him from where return would have been impossible.

A few days later, a call from Stella's father about the disclosure of a psychiatrist's hypnotism report and the necessity for a shock treatment as Stella had been diagnosed with schizophrenia, further immersed Vincent into a sea of anguish and mortification. He cursed himself for not having acted promptly when she had complained about the immediate neighbour's attempts to scandalise and harass her. Night shifts made it impossible for Vincent to investigate if there was any element of truth in her allegations. He could not be the caring husband he should have been as he caught up on lost sleep during the day.

The Nairs came across as sociable and friendly people when Vincent moved with his family next door to them. Relationships took an ugly turn with differences of opinion, suspicion and petty quarrels. Mrs. Nair, who was an unattractive, dark complexioned and a very small person, was jealous of Stella's fair complexion, feminine grace and traditional beauty. As she regarded Stella as a threat to her ill-matched, insecure marital relationship, in Vincent's absence, she gathered a few tenants under the portico of her house, which was adjacent to Stella's bedroom, and verbally abused her in her booming voice. Stella's pleas for intervention fell on deaf, disbelieving ears and being emotionally sensitive, the impact of recurrent abuse led to sleeplessness and the beginning stages of schizophrenia. Vincent regretted his insensitivity; his only excuse being his ignorance. If he had known neglect would lead to disastrous consequences, he would have been proactive.

For order to be restored at home, until Stella returned, Vincent sought the assistance of his mother who cooked, cleaned, ensured Neha went to school regularly and provided him the guidance and counselling he desperately needed. Stella returned home after three months' treatment at SCARF, Chennai but was not the person the family had known. Insensitive comments mistaken for rudeness and anti-social personality became a regular phenomenon with her.

Vincent's mother returned to Kerala and Stella resumed her wifely and motherly duties and within days' normalcy returned. Constant medication and periodic consultancy with a psychiatrist became mandatory for her wellbeing.

* * *

'Right turn?' the query of the taxi driver interrupted her thought stream and she returned to the present with a jolt only to mechanically direct the taxi-driver to a cluster of strata maintained two-storeyed villas, which elicited a delightful gasp from the passengers.

The uniformity in the structure and pleasant colours of the villas was overshadowed by an unexplained callousness, which could only be sensed by long term dwellers.

Time stands for none and for Neha it flew rather too quickly with trips to popular landmarks. Sydney Harbour Bridge and Opera House topping the long list, coupled with shopping sprees and dining-out evenings. There were moments of understandings and misunderstandings which suspended the vacuum Neha experienced in her life after her divorce, and which even though did not strengthen the familial bonds, failed to tarnish the joy evoked by the experience of togetherness. There were moments when Neha and George had nowhere to escape but to confront each other with issues that had developed into bitterness with the passage of time.

'When Dad was losing his life to pancreatic cancer, I know I was not the devoted daughter or the supportive sister that you desired me to be,' said Neha knowingly.

Looking directly at George who pretended to be disinterested she continued, 'I was caught up in bickering and dissensions that were predecessors to divorce. I was in an emotional turmoil and incapable of making any rational decision and providing moral support to any one let alone you.'

George's disappointment and sourness stemmed from the fact that not only did he have to sacrifice his savings for over-inflated hospital expenses but he was also mentally exhausted.

'I desperately wanted you to be there by my side. There were things I believed I could not share with Mona but only with you because we grew up together, we understood the politics within the family and we knew Dad like the back of our hands,' responded George in an emotionally laden voice.

Ensuring that he had Neha's undivided attention he continued, 'You left me in a lurch when you did not show up for our father's funeral ceremony and abandoned me in my greatest moment of need. I bore the brunt of criticism and coped the embarrassment of having to explain to friends and family why you could not make it for the funeral.'

Neha defended her choices and decisions but she was not sure if George could fathom the enormity of her predicament. She still gave it a try.

'With an Apprehended Violence Order in place and a court summons, I was struggling with mortgage payments, credit card charges, utility bills and contention in the workplace. Expiry of John's passport did not ameliorate the situation at all.'

She added, 'You think it is easy to get a signature for a new passport from Prem, who was uncooperative in every way? He would have flatly refused. I could not leave John behind and travel alone as I did not have friends whom I could really trust.'

Even though their attempts to patch their differences were not triumphant, Neha and George were willing to put things behind them for the happiness of the family. Neha was glad to observe that

George was having the time of his life, which he captured digitally, shared and Facebooked. There were moments when gratitude was expressed, which purged all negativity from the reunion making it a memorable one, worth cherishing. Her family's departure after their brief visit did not leave her devastated or emotional as she had assumed. On the contrary, she felt detached and impalpable from sentiments associated with relationships. Like mother, like daughter?

SEVEN

HUNTED

Sporting activities lost its original excitement for John, especially after he had packed a few pounds in the span of a few months, which explained his preference to absent himself on such days. Ever since they had moved to Canley Heights, John did not pursue his dreams of becoming a cricket player and neither did he long to become a soccer player, which could have been one of the contributing reasons for his obesity. Even though he pretended body image was not a pressing issue, there were days when he returned teary-eyed and down in spirits from school due to psychologically depressing remarks passed by immature, thoughtless and vindictive students. Neha allowed John to stay at home on such occasions as she did not want self-esteem issues to maim him emotionally. The knowledge that even the most effective bullying policies of schools failed to protect a student, whose difference attracted unwanted attention and scarring comments, influenced Neha's decision to support John's choice.

'I am allowing you to stay home on the conditions that you complete your assignments and keep your book work up-to-date for the subjects we agreed upon yesterday,' repeated Neha a third time.

'Okay mum. I will do my work. I promise.' 'Will you give me the HDMI cable when you come back from work?' asked John suspiciously.

'That depends. These days XBox One means everything to you. You should attach more importance to learning and exercising rather than gaming, which is only for entertainment. Be a good boy. I must go. I am running late. I will see you in the afternoon,' replied Neha giving a quick hug and a kiss before she darted out of the door.

While wading through the heavy traffic, she reflected on the evils of technology and how disobedience, indiscipline and inappropriate language were the side effects of an overdose of gaming. It being 'Activities Week' a few minutes lateness would not matter Neha thought especially as she had opted for Gardening activities, which was organised at school.

The students were busy painting the shelters a little after 10:00 am in the morning when the shocking news of a hostage siege at Lindt Chocolat café in Martin Place in Sydney by jihadist Man Haron Monis caused quite a furore as the safety of teachers and students, who had travelled to the city, had to be ascertained. The temporary suspension of public transportation, especially trains, made it impossible for them to reach the venues of planned activities. Those stuck on trains returned after coping two to three hours of immovability. Those who were fortunate to have reached their venues were apprehensive about returning to school before the closing time as anxious and agitated parents were not often easy to deal with.

A tumultuous day at school drained Neha of her energy and left her with a pounding headache. John was waiting expectantly at the door for his cable. By using the cable to connect the console to the TV, he was hoping to create an image of a tech-savvy gamer, who was as insanely skilled as any professional player.

'Did you finish all the work?' asked Neha.

'Yes mum,' answered John impatiently while continuing the conversation with some virtual friend on the other end of the headset.

Neha applied some balm to her head before she sipped her tea and dug into the snacks that she had laid out for John earlier in the day. She quickly scanned through the pages of John's exercise books and although not satisfied with the quality of the work, did not breathe a word to him for two obvious reasons. It was never a good idea to talk to him while he was preoccupied as it usually resulted in overhead transmission. Her headache had zapped her off the energy to engage in a masterly argument, for often the outcome was negative, as it did not produce the much-yearned-for-improvement. Unable to withstand the intensity of the pain, she prostrated herself on the black three-seater leather lounge, rested her head on the zebra patterned sofa cushions and wished desperately for a miraculous relief, which came as a siesta.

Sleep-laden eyelids struggled to open when Neha became suddenly aware of an invasion within her inner lips and her eyelids flew open rapidly with fear clutching her heart, in an extraordinary grip, as she was unable to comprehend the unexpected phenomenon. She turned sharply to her left, where her son was seated comfortably on a two-seater black leather lounge copiously engaged in the use of gaming jargon while conversing with his virtual friend, blissfully unaware of his mother's apprehension. The slow movement swiftly transformed into deliberately purposeful strokes of a sensual nature, which left Neha baffled as she was a neophyte. An invisible infiltration was contrary to the passionate intercourse she was accustomed to, which though left her feeling mauled, fulfilled her insatiable craving, which ranged between lust and love and contented in the knowledge that she was desired.

Neha coerced herself to sit upright on the sofa before she busied herself with domestic chores, with dinner preparations gaining priority on her list.

'What's for dinner?' called out John from the living room which never failed to amuse Neha, who could not dispense with the thought that he had a watch on his tummy.

'How about tuna balls?' queried Neha.

'That's my fav mum. Thanks mum,' responded John offhandedly and continued in the lingo that Neha deemed gibberish.

'So, what are you cooking luv?' questioned a sinister voice from the inner ears in an attempt to initiate conversation. Neha almost threw the potatoes that she was peeling in to the air and rescued it from scattering on the floor by intercepting it in the eventuali momenti. With a sharp intake of breath, she quickly scrutinized the room to see if she was entertained by unwanted, intimidating company. She thought she was hallucinating as she could not detect the presence of anyone in the kitchenette. She quickly dismissed the uncomfortable thought and realised that she would need a larger bowl to resume with the mixing of potatoes and seasoned tuna before she could roll them into balls, dip them in egg, coat them in bread crumbs and deep fry in oil.

Neha busied herself with washing the dishwashing liquid off a spacious stainless steel bowl when she could have sworn that she felt her neck being grabbled and her fuller bottom lip sucked or chewed on. Kissed by a mystical anonymity, Neha stood motionless and breathless trapped between illusion and reality. She waited for a recurrence of the incident, however, disappointed, resumed dinner preparations.

'John, what sauce would you like to have with the tuna balls?' bellowed out Neha as she was laying out four crispy golden brown balls on to a circular porcelain plate.

'Sweet chilly,' called out John as he was turning the console off and winding the wire of his headset around the two earphones.

'Make sure you pack your school bag according to the timetable before you go to bed,' commanded Neha, who hated the morning delays with a vengeance.

'I am going upstairs to change the sheets and when you finish all your work here you can come upstairs,' said Neha cheerfully.

She pulled out the soiled sheets and replaced them with fresh linen that fanned out detergent fragrance, which tickled her sensitive nostrils. Within few minutes, pyjama attired John entered the en-suite with a Shweppes Lemonade bottle filled with water for the night.

Neha tucked him in with a breezy 'G'night', switched off the tube light and tiptoed out of the room into the adjoining bedroom.

Neha tossed and turned in her bed with her fitful sleep depleting rather than invigorating her when she thought she saw a dark hand. Enervation known to have played strange tricks on many a sleep deprived homo sapiens spared no mercy on her too, thought Neha to cajole herself. Simultaneously, unable to dispense the gnawing fear growing within her, she invoked the gods with eyes shut tightly. Each time the hand caressed her or fondled her, Neha stiffened and shuddered and the soft lewd whispers did not mitigate her anxiety.

Toilet flush sounds awakened Neha the next morning. She struggled to recollect when she surrendered herself to the soothing comfort of slumber but in vain. Having overslept, Neha was displeased with herself as she had to rush things to avoid lateness. She could not stop herself from retorting to the voices, who were engaged in irrelevant conversations, in her mind, fearful of coming across as schizophrenic or a raving lunatic to John. Her vexation knew no bounds when her choices were interfered with or commands contrary to the dictates of common sense were prompted.

'Mum, can you help me with the shoe laces?' pleaded John.

'Let me get the car out of the garage and I will be with you soon,' said Neha as she opened the shutters of the garage.

'John, you are old enough to tie your own shoe laces. You should learn to cross the loops and knot the laces this weekend,' advised Neha when she reached his side.

'I know mum. I will,' replied John in a disheartened manner.

'There you are! Cheer up. Now be a good boy and wait for me in the car. Remember to take the school bag with you. I'll join you when I turn on the alarm and finish locking the doors,' instructed Neha.

In two minutes, she clambered into the car and cautiously reversed the car from the driveway onto the road before accelerating it to speed limit recommended in residential areas. The voices and intrusions would have to wait as she had to focus on driving safely.

Neha waved a kiss and a goodbye to her son, which was followed by an enthusiastic, 'Have a nice day!' when she dropped him off at the suburban high school, which was speedily met by John's, 'You too mum'.

Driving in solitude, Neha realised that the voices chose to accompany her wherever she went. She was furious that she was touched, fondled, squeezed and invaded against her wishes but it became increasingly difficult to ignore the pleasurable sensations the moves precipitated as the organs were designed for that very purpose.

'How is this possible?' wondered Neha.

The inconspicuousness or invisibility that shrouded the mysterious manhandling, which she preferred to term harassment for unknown reasons, was beyond her comprehension.

The familiar and unfamiliar voices' interference during teaching was resisted by Neha, who adamantly ignored the conversations, and persevered with following her own mind. Initially the harassment was more sexual as in she received gratification at frequent periodic intervals, however, it took an ugly turn when she was away from school to attend professional development courses. She felt it was the handiwork of an illusionist, who made her feel that different sizes of dildo shaped objects were inserted into her, with an enhancement in size each time. She sat through the sessions expressionless, adjusting her sitting position to mask the discomfort she was experiencing and to prevent her legs from becoming numb, paralysed. She was convinced that the harassers' intentions were not honourable as the emphasis was more on incapacitating her from work rather than sensual indulgence.

Days and nights and months passed and the tormentors tirelessly taunted Neha physically and mentally causing sleep deprivation hoping to reduce her to the status of a psychological wreck. Divine intervention came to Neha in the form of an undefeatable, unflinching spirit that chose to be defiant rather than succumb and despite being subjected to twenty-four-hour surveillance, though highly doubtful, she did not cringe even from inspection in the nude. Rumours and deliberate comments made it impossible for Neha to dismiss the occurrences as a figment of imagination.

During a lesson, a teacher led discussion touched upon the subject of psychology.

'Mrs. Prem I was watching a TV series and the detective used hypnotism to find out if he had committed the crime,' stated a student with enthusiasm.

Another butted in with, 'You know these days, criminals can even deceive a lie detector and I wonder if he confessed the truth when hypnotised.'

'That clearly proves that one method of investigation can never be relied upon,' added Neha, who was glad to see how the students were engaged and eager to contribute to the class discussion.

'Well, one thing is clear that the police/CIA/CID whatever you call them have tried innumerable ways to control the minds of the criminals for whatever reason,' finished a very silent, observant student.

The words 'mind control' had a strange impact on Neha, who thought the pieces of a messed-up puzzle were eventually falling into place. 'That's it. Mind games!' whispered Neha to herself. People, near and distant from her, were trying to control her thoughts, actions and emotions by monitoring her movements. Conversations from films, between relatives and her own conversations with friends and foes were recorded and replayed to confuse her mind. Neha could not wait to reach home to research on mind control. On her way home, Neha picked up John from the take away shops where he usually waited. Once inside the car he said, 'Mum I need some help with Multimedia assignment.'

'No problem. I will let you use the computer after I finish my work. I have something important to research,' responded Neha excitedly.

'Mum, we need Adobe Illustrator to finish the work,' stated John.

'Oh! You can use the DET laptop. It has Adobe software or programs like Photoshop and other things. Don't worry John, I am sure we can come up with something,' comforted Neha.

Neha parked her car in the garage as she was determined to use time effectively to get to the bottom of the mind games rather than waste her time in shopping. She logged on to the computer, with a steaming cup of coffee next to her on the computer table waiting to be sipped. Her eyes were arrested by an interesting article on Nano implant microchip devices published by MindTech (World CACH) Sweden. The similarities in experiences pinpointed by the article were astounding and mindboggling. There were times when Neha suspected that those around her read her thoughts as fast as she formed them; like they were reading automated captions on a computer screen. There were occasions when she was distracted by voice transmissions through electronic objects near her. There were nights when Neha's sleep was disturbed by sounds of a person skateboarding on the adjacent roads or people attempting to break in to the property and on waking up had gone back to repose realising that it was untrue. She could not find answers to the questions that had popped up in her head several times in the recent months, 'Why are they doing this to me? Why am I being hunted? Am I a terrorist? Am I a criminal?'

'If there was an involuntary microchip within my body, how and when was it implanted?' Neha wondered with alarm.

'Who was responsible for this? How am I going to get the rice-grain sized silicone microchip removed as the process of locating it was difficult and expensive?' thought Neha, alarmed at the magnitude of her predicament.

She could not help recalling a recently viewed YouTube clip titled 'Mind Control – Remote Neural Monitoring' in which Daniel Estulin interviewed Magnus Olsson, whose article she had stumbled upon unintentionally while researching. She pondered if the Indian or the Australian government had any specific reason for making her the targeted individual.

The unresolved ending of the article increased her apprehension as she was powerless to discontinue the touching, fondling, caressing and invading. She desperately hoped that time would overwrite the chip and deactivate it. Determined not to be paranoid or phobic, she pursued varied survival strategies that would assist her in challenging the functions of the microchip and emerge unharmed.

EIGHT

REMINISCENCES

The name of the Indian city of Tamilnadu state may not resonate as anything significant to multitudes, however, it had an indefinable significance to Neha whose carefree childhood and tumultuous teenage years were shaped by the vivacious, crowded, multicultural, urban agglomeration. When Neha's birth was celebrated in Mehta Hospital, Chennai by her grandparents, aunts and uncles, the regime of Indian National Congress in Tamilnadu was terminated by the rising popularity of DMK with M.K. Karunanidhi holding the office of Chief Minister. Brooke Bond Tea Company, where her father was employed, lost their British ipseity and gained an Anglo-Dutch identity with Unilever's annexation. Neha was introduced to Kovai, when her new mother was allowed to join her life partner after a confinement period of sixty days during which she was nurtured and pampered as per South Indian traditions. Ever since, Kovai had been a trusted companion in her life who brought frolic, magic and romance to her formative years; a silent witness to her tales of joy and sorrow, who was never reluctant to offer a shoulder to cry.

Transition occurred not only in Neha's life. Kovai also transitioned from sweltering summers with extreme temperatures as high as 40 degrees, to monsoon madness with the heavy downpour drenching everyone and everything in her line of approach, to not so chilly romantic winters offering a pleasant relief to weather-beaten residents. Princess birthdays with precious gifts from loved ones, family movie night at KG cinema complex or Central and Kanakadhara theatres, dining out with family at Hotel Sree Annapoorna and Ananda Bhavan, family dinners at friends or relatives' residences added zest to her colour-filled childhood days. Waterfalls, temples, shopping complexes, textile and engineering industries and educational institutions transformed Kovai to an iconic city not only in the state but also in the country.

1970's was a time when English medium schools left such a distinctive impression in the field of education that middle-class parents with unexceptional income clamoured for admissions in private schools even before the birth of their offsprings. One occasion when catholicity genuinely assisted parents was when obtaining a spot for their children at catholic schools despite intense competition. Neha's pursuit for a successful career commenced in 1978 when she was enrolled at Avila Convent Matriculation Higher Secondary School, Coimbatore. Oblivious to the economic stress her education was initiating in her father, Neha reaped the rewards of a seed that her father had sown.

As a student, she remembered how she welcomed festivals

wholeheartedly as they brought additional holidays besides the calendared school vacations. Diwali, Pongal, Saraswati Puja, Ayudha Puja, Muharram, Ramzan and Christmas filled the city and the streets of her district with magic as decorations, lights and fireworks beautified the edifices rendering them supernal. Taste buds were tickled by the variety of homemade ghee-fragrant sweets and savouries that good-natured neighbours attired in new ethnic and fashionable outfits brought home with immense pleasure.

Entering the threshold of adolescence, Neha found herself intrigued by a fascinating subject that was not offered at the catholic school for secondary students, boys. She had failed to appreciate their company when she studied with them till Fourth Standard in the primary until the nuns, who were intolerant to indiscipline, plotted and schemed and eventually bid farewell to them. She had always found her male counterparts annoying, maliciously ridiculing and unfriendly material whose presence should be avoided. She had an unmistakable memory of having pushed a boy, who was standing on the desk with such anger and force, that when he stood up after a heavy fall he was the bearer of a chipped tooth. Bodily changes, hormonal development and pubescence transfigured those irksome lads suddenly into attractive species, whose attention was worth craving.

Neha basked in the glory of her secret admirers and audacious ones, who dared to disregard societal restrictions, and advance a proposition that lasted until she burst their bubble. Boys in the neighbourhood, from adjacent schools, who eyed pretty or smart looking girls from bakeries, shops and bus stops in the proximity of the catholic school, at church, in Sunday catechism classes, participating in rotary club events, at function venues, at popular eateries and so ran the seemingly endless list. They were an irresistible topic to converse with her girlfriends in hushed voices within the privacy of her room that often-generated excitement, which overruled apprehensions of being overheard by eavesdropping family members. Harlequin, Silhouette romance and Mills and Boon series were read voraciously as Neha did not have access to internet cafes, which were made available to the public only in 1995. Every girl had a crush on some boy somewhere at some time as though it was an unspoken law in the adolescent kingdom. Like every other girl, Neha survived those temporary distractions until HSC state board exams.

It was customary for 12th Standard students in the 1990's to sit for the state board exams in external venues. Avila Convent Matriculation Higher Secondary school and a few other local schools had their venue as Sri Avinashilingam Home Science College for women, which had acquired the status of 'Deemed University' three years ago; a venue where Neha's resolve to be solitary was no match against the unfathomable power of the Sisters of Fate. On the final day of her board exams, Neha heaved a sigh of relief as she walked to the bus stop thinking about the umpteen number of things she could pursue with pleasure during her long vacation, when a stranger's intense gaze discontinued her thoughts.

He strode with confidence towards her and said, 'Hey beautiful, what's your name? I am Prem.'

Neha pondered in silence if she should engage in a conversation with a total stranger.

Noticing the year 12 text books she was tightly clutching he asked, 'How did you find your exams?'

Reluctantly she responded in a barely audible voice, 'I did okay I guess. By the way I am Neha. Glad to meet you.'

Neha glanced slyly at this audacious admirer, who was

different from other boys she had known. He was a tall, chocolate-complexioned, South Indian looking young man whose robust glow and side-partitioned, layered, straight dark hair flicked backwards stirred a hitherto never experienced fluttering feeling in the pit of her stomach.

She could sense his growing boldness as he queried, 'Whereabouts do you live? I have seen you a few times from the window of moving buses in the Simpson Nagar area. There were times when I longed to jump out of the moving bus just to strike a conversation with you.'

Suppressing a smile, she cautiously replied, 'I live in the residential area of the Nagar. Where do you live?'

His reply was drowned in the noise around them as they had reached the bus stop, which was directly in front of the second gate of the university, from where hundreds of students spilled out chattering excitedly of how easy they had found the last paper and conjecturing the high scores they would procure if the marking was not too strict.

Neha repeated her question to which Prem replied in a raised voice, 'Chinnathadagam'.

Her perplexed look confirmed that her geographical knowledge of the area was not impressive. She heard a deep throaty chuckle, which was strangely seductive. When she noticed the smear of sacred ashes on his forehead, the excitement building within her turned into dismay.

In a melancholic tone, she interrogated, 'Are you a Hindu? I am a Christian. Roman Catholic.' She was unsuccessful in masking the disappointment in her voice and she sensed Prem standing before her and gazing into her eyes clouded with confusion.

'So, what?' he demanded.

'You are modern in the way you dress but not in your thoughts,' he mused.

His evaluation infuriated Neha. She wished that society shared his inter-religious utopian ideology. She liked him and wanted to learn more about him and his world, however, she could not bear the thought of parting in bitterness. She yearned to capture the chance encounter in an immortal moment like Keats' lovers on the Grecian Urn.

When the bus screeched to a halt, Neha moved with an agility that surprised Prem and boarded the bus before he could stop her. A frozen image, immersed in anguish and confoundment haunted her mind's eye, for the next few months.

The Sisters of Fate conspired and threw the fated lovers into sister institutions, which heightened the possibility of the couple meeting each other. They did. Neha caught sight of Prem waiting for public transport from the window of Bus no: 16A. From the corner of her eye, she observed his mannerisms while he interacted with few young men, who she presumed to be his friends. When she realised that she was shamelessly staring at him, she looked away but it was too late as he had spotted her. Like a scene from a Bollywood film, her heart skipped a beat sans the romantic melodious background music. She heard the conductor ring the bell, which was the cue for the bus operator to resume the journey via the designated route. Her private thoughts were interrupted by a familiar voice, which made her eyes search frantically for its possessor, among the sea of passengers in the overcrowded bus at peak time. Her eyes did not have to trail far as they locked with Prem's piercing gaze from which she had to tear hers away. The Sisters of Fate celebrated their success as a scandalous affair was born.

In a South Indian orthodox society, two and a half decades ago when dating was a taboo, when love affairs were surreptitious and when unlawful relationships before marriage tarnished character, Neha and Prem chose to rebel against existing norms by publicising their amorous relationship. What was covert initially with their day meetings at ice-cream parlours, cinemas, airport gradually progressed into bold dusk rendezvous. Prem picked up Neha from the local typewriting institute after her lesson and drove into the dusky maize fields far from the madding crowd, just to melt into each other's embrace, passionately kiss and quiver in pleasure with each other's touch. Weeks became months and months became years and the couple continued to be the talk of the town, survivors of religious bigotry and subject of wild whispers and raging rumours. Neha and Prem's motorbike rides were not an uncommon sight for Coimbatoreans.

Seven years of courtship advanced into a Christian wedding at Little Flower Church, Saibaba colony; an event that attracted the battalion of relatives and friends as it was the first inter-caste marriage in the family and a much talked about dalliance. Reception followed the wedding ceremony as was customary after which Neha and Prem, contrary to the families' expectations, vamoosed into their humble abode to enjoy conjugal bliss. Being employees of self-financing institutions, they were compelled to resume work as they were only allowed a short break. Neha slipped in to the position of a weekend wife with her first government appointment at a hill station, four hours away from Tirupur, ruling out the possibility of daily travel back and forth.

Amidst this hectic schedule, Neha and Prem, as a newlywed couple, followed the traditions of paying a visit to all the close relatives' dwellings in Kerala for lunch or dinner, the outcome of which was mostly favourable as language barrier posed the least of complications with most being able to converse in English. Neha found Prem's smile, nod and play along tactics while conversing with the elderly to compensate for the language deficiency, hilarious. It was visits to Neha's parents' home that stirred up a hornet's nest as Prem was conscious of his cultural differences and realised that he would never gain total acceptance that a Christian, Malayalee son-in-law would.

'I couldn't sleep well last night,' he stated while returning from Neha's parents' home.

'Why?' interrogated Neha.

'Well, there were no mosquito repellent incense coils. A mosquito net would have helped.'

'Why do have to complain about silly issues? Is it hard to adjust for one night?' retorted Neha angrily, sticking up for her parents as most loyal daughters would.

'In our culture, the wife's family would treat their son-in-law as the king and give him all the importance,' he added.

'Why didn't you marry from your culture then ha? You were not being exactly cooperative. During family prayer time, my dad included you as a family member and all you could do was sit in the chair and look towards the window when you could have turned the chair in the direction of god's image,' said Neha all flared up.

'I joined the prayer. Isn't that enough?' asked Prem unperturbed by Neha's raging temper.

'Joined? I think you were humiliating us. You should have been prepared for obstacles when you decided in favour of love marriage. Now you want the privileges of an arranged marriage, don't you? Don't forget that you are married to me and not to my parents!' shouted Neha before she retreated into stony silence.

Bickering based on in-laws' actions and behaviour were not

uncommon between husbands and wives. Arguments of such nature usually erected a temporary wall between couples that mended with the passage of time. However, such wrangling left Neha with a sense of impending doom.

NINE

CRUMBLED

'What do you think about sharing the expenses equally?' asked Prem cautiously.

'Why? We have been able to get along ten years without doing so. Is there anything I should know?' inquired Neha in a sharp voice.

'I have been paying the mortgage for the property for five years now. You refuse to contribute any amount to the combined savings account, which was offered as part of the ANZ Break Free Home loan package. I cannot do it on my own,' said Prem vexed at Neha's reaction.

'We have been through this a few times in the recent weeks. You agreed to pay the mortgage as I was working as a casual teacher when we bought the house. You were the permanent employee of CityRail, remember? Don't overlook my contributions. Look around the house. I paid for every piece of furniture and electronic white goods you are using,' pointed out Neha.

'All I'm saying is that if we add all our expenses, including utility bills, and divide them between us things could be convenient for both of us and we will be able to keep the ball rolling,' finished off Prem in a rush anticipating an outburst.

'Is this some game you are playing because I am now a full time permanent staff at the school? Who has been paying child care fees from day one? It's not cheap let me tell you. I pay approximately $150 per week, even with the government rebate. Each time you invite your friends over, I rush to Woollies and buy everything necessary for the parties including alcohol. I have never asked you to reimburse the bills,' retorted Neha in a raised voice.

'This is what I don't like about you. Every time I try to have a conversation, you start shouting and screaming. Lower your voice. If you deposit your pay in to the combined account the interest would be low,' stated Prem.

'Now you have problems with my voice. What else do you have problems with? You might as well say it now than later. Whenever we go for dinners and birthday parties, I buy gifts for their children. Expensive gifts, mind you. If I deposit into the combined account does that not give you the right to withdraw anytime you want without my consent? I would not be able to stop you, would I?' sneered Neha.

'Don't you trust me? Who has been supporting you all these years? So now you have become all worldly wise? I was the one who brought you to Australia. It would be useful to remember that next time you want to give me attitude,' said Prem through ground teeth.

'Let's not go there. I leased my house for the ticket and other expenses. So, you did not spend your money to bring me here. I paid for my passage and yours for that matter. I cannot cancel my Commonwealth bank account because I have a car loan and a credit card with them,' remarked Neha in a tone that hinted that she was on the brink of losing patience.

'Where was the need to buy that second-hand car? I told you not to go for it. You never follow my advice. I want you to seriously consider sharing the expenses,' Prem expressed his views in a stern voice.

'You would know if you were a casual. I receive a call between 8:00 and 8:30 am and by the time I reach the school using public transport I am late. You know what that means? The school would not contact me a second time. When I asked you to give me few lessons in your car, you were not exactly co-operative. I had to pay the driving instructor for all the required hours. If I don't own a car I would not be able to work on my driving skills. What's the point of passing the driving test?' observed Neha contemptuously.

She continued, 'I know what's going on. Haven't you heard of the maxim "Faults are thick when love is thin". Why would you feel compelled to hold on to half your earnings? What could be more important to you than John and me? Do your parents need financial assistance? If that's the case, you just have to say so.'

Prem responded, 'No they don't need our money. My father is paying your home loan and the insurance in India, with his retirement money, as we are not able to afford both the mortgage payments. You don't understand...' his voice trailed off.

As Neha saw John approaching them after his short nap she added, 'By the way I spend for John's clothes, shoes, books and all his exclusive character toys and action figurines. Unless you tell me what the real reason is I am not going to agree to splitting all the bills equally. End of conversation,' she concluded the argument emphatically.

Neha turned to John and asked, 'Did you have a good sleep?' to which he nodded in the affirmative.

'Then you must be feeling hungry,' she said with a smile.

John in his half wakeful state nodded again while struggling to sit on the two seater Crosby fabric sofa with his legs crossed. Neha switched on the television and played his favourite film 'Madagascar: Escape 2 Africa', which he never grew tired of viewing. Before darting into the kitchen to get some warm milk and cookies for John, she gave a quick scan from the living room to see what Prem was distracting himself with. Through the faded white venetian blinds of the living room window, she saw him engaged in deep conversation with someone on the phone. She thought it was unusual for him to pace around the recently mowed lawns while attempting to, what seemed to her, as pacifying a not-so-happy individual on the other end. John's excited laughter interrupted her observations and she proceeded to the kitchen.

That day's discord was just the beginning to be followed by many others. Without prior consultation, a friend and his wife was invited for mediation; a move which Neha resented bitterly as the emphasis once again was on dividing the expenses, and the denouement of the conciliation was predictably unpleasant. A few weeks later, convinced that she would not be incurring any loss, eventually, when she conceded to split the bills equally between them, things failed to improve. When he walked through the entrance of the property after his rostered shift, he wore an expression of abhorrence that could not be dismissed as insignificant as it became a regular practice. Public humiliation while socializing with friends was adopted as a strategy to ruffle Neha's feathers, which on occasions she bore silently, and on other times, she responded with volatile reactions.

During one of the late-night parties, Prem suddenly whisked John off to Neha's car and drove off without offering any explanation while she was half way through her dinner. She had one too many glasses of wine that night and was conscious that any reaction from her would be interpreted as alcohol induced behaviour. She finished her dinner calmly, thanked the hosts for a delicious meal, and as the heavily intoxicated host was barely able to offer a lift home, she stumbled out of the house at midnight into the street lamp lit roads of the residential area of Ingleburn. Masking her fear of any unknown dangers that she suspected to be lurking in the darkness, she steadied her gait and continued briskly not stopping once until she reached her destination, which fortunately was at a walkable distance. On reaching her driveway, Neha retrieved the keys from the car, which was left unlocked, and let herself into her home only to retire for the night.

No plausible elucidation was provided the next morning. Pleas for esteem fell on deaf ears. A point was reached in life when situations could not be salvaged. Harassed repeatedly for divorce for reasons unknown, Neha severed ties with all mutual friends. John was a silent observer during most of the heated exchanges, which convinced him at an early age that his father who was responsible for his mother's anguish and disgrace, deserved no allegiance.

On a sultry summer evening, Prem broke the uncanny silence only to declare calmly to Neha, 'I want you to find a lawyer and make arrangements for a divorce.'

Neha replied dispassionately, 'If you are desperate for a divorce why can't you make the arrangements yourself.'

Vanquished in his immediate goal, which was to hold Neha

responsible for the impending divorce, he resorted to excessive drinking every day irrespective of the time his shift ended. Prem would return with take away food from restaurants or fast food centers, shower, change into jammies, settle on the three-seater fabric sofa, not before laying out the food on the table with a glass of whisky in his hands, and entertain himself with his favourite Indian movies. Neha ignored his existence in the house focusing on her motherly and professional duties. He tried everything in his capacity to force her to take the first step towards divorce but his efforts proved futile.

One fateful day, Prem announced his intentions to take the family to Cabramatta. Neha wondered what had caused the change in attitude as he had planned a family outing. She agreed to go as he expressed his desire to buy John his favourite things. Little did she know that she was a pawn in his master plan. On reaching the bustling crowded streets of the suburb that guaranteed a taste of Asia, Prem found a parking spot in Dutton Lane car park. He escorted Neha and John into a solicitor's office located on the second floor of an old narrow dingy double storeyed building. When they stepped into the reception area with files stacked all-round the desk and a few chairs and a double seater sofa claiming the remaining space in the room, a young Chinese woman gestured to them to step into the adjacent room.

A Vietnamese looking attorney looked up from the file he was scrutinizing, greeted them and indicated them to take their seats.

When they were comfortably seated at his table, skipping the formalities of introduction, Prem asked the attorney, 'Are the divorce papers ready?'

A dagger descended into her heavy chest. A tear stung her eye before it rolled down her cheek. A lump in her throat stole her words.

A proud woman was reborn. Redeeming the remnants of her lost dignity, she quietly stretched her hand out for the documents. Life ebbed out of her as she scrawled her signature on the freshly printed divorce papers. The deed was done.

'Could we discuss the terms of the settlement? There could be a tidy sum. You could be surprised,' prompted the solicitor.

'I do not want anything,' said Neha defiantly as she rose from her seat.

Blinded with tears, she grabbed John by the hand and stepped outside the building quickly for fresh air. Her constricted throat was choking her. She had just managed to swallow back her tears when Prem joined her and John. Wasted youth and meaningless sacrifices mocked and plagued her as she followed Prem, who was determined to do some shopping before they left for their home that had nightmarishly transitioned into a house.

A game of chess in which Neha had failed to checkmate the king first when opportunities presented themselves to her. Prem's words, 'sometimes to achieve prosperity one has to adapt to deception,' echoed in her ears. Her efforts to transfer the jointly owned house solely into her name were beaten as Prem refused to sign the financial agreement prepared in consultation with lawyers, despite obtaining pre-approval for home loan in her name from Commonwealth bank. Paying someone else's mortgage was not her idea of progress, especially if the chances of becoming a sole owner was impossible. She became a question mark. An unfinished puzzle. An intricate crossword. An impervious shooting star yet to determine her course.

TEN

DEPARTED

The pitter patter of rain, the howling winds and the chillness of winter on a mid-June night added bleakness to her uneventful Sunday night, when the ringtone of the landline shattered the silence in the living room. Neha had just switched off the television ruminating on the unfair victimisation of Kevin Rudd by Labor party's coup led by Julia Gillard and was about to kill the lights, when the phone rang. In a few strides, she picked up the receiver and was relieved to recognise her brother's voice at the other end.

'Neha?' asked George.

'Yes. Thank god, it's you. I was wondering who the caller could be.'

George continued in a serious tone, 'Be calm. What I am going to tell you might unsettle you but you know we have all been anticipating this. What I mean is ... it is not sudden or unexpected. Dad passed away this evening.'

Neha was dumbfounded. Her eyes moistened as images of her father swam before her mind's eye.

George asked, 'Are you there?'

'I am here... When is the funeral?'

'We can't keep the body for days as he was a cancer patient. It is day after tomorrow,' informed George.

'I won't be attending. I am sorry. I am not in a situation to travel immediately. That's all I can say,'

'Oh! I had to face everything on my own. Relatives are not going to be silent. You know that, don't you? I am busy with the preparations for the ceremony. Mona has been informing friends and family. Even if I leave one relative out, there is bound to be tongue lashing,' said George in a voice that betrayed his frustration.

'I have my reasons. It has not been easy for me to go through divorce on my own,'

George became emotional when he reflected, 'I feel crippled without Dad. I did not realise how much I depended on him for guidance. It is true that we fail to realise a person's value when he/she is with us, isn't it?'

'I know how you feel. I wish I can be there for you. I really am sorry.'

George philosophised before he ended the call, 'Fate plays strange tricks with our lives. I will talk to you after the ceremony. Take care.'

With a heavy heart, Neha made her way to the bedroom where John was fast asleep. She tucked him in and lay beside him as he was scared to sleep alone. The house was unusually silent at night and the absence of his father made him feel very insecure. Prem lived as a tenant in Glenfield in a mutual friend's house ever since the AVO came into effect. He had failed to pay the mortgage instalments and the bank sent letters to Neha asking her to catch up with the payments as she was a joint owner. She used up her limited savings to keep her loan up-to-date. And there were other issues which made it impossible for her to just pack and leave for Kerala to attend her father's funeral. She became one of those innumerable settlers, whom families never expected to show up.

Neha realised that she was sobbing when memories of her father swarmed into her mind. She thought that George was right about her father always being there for them. Things changed when she showed independence, failed to value the father-daughter relationship above all others, and disappointed him by her less discreet choices, which projected him as an incapable parent. She remembered fondly how he would wake up just to make her some tea and then fall back asleep while she pursued her early morning study routines for HSC exams. She could not forget how he ran down eight flight of stairs to photocopy few certificates that were expedient for a government employment interview, which she was about to attend in few minutes. She left him struggling from shortness of breath, mild chest pain and soaking in excessive perspiration to attend the interview without realising that those were the early symptoms of a cardiac arrest.

Few months later, she had to cut short her vacation at her uncle's place to be by Vincent's side as he was hospitalised due to a mild heart attack, which required a Coronary Angioplasty. Six months later when Vincent had a major arrest, by-pass surgery became inevitable. On both occasions, she recalled how her heart went out to the bedridden, frail and defenseless man, whose sacrifices developed her professional and personal identity. Even though he recovered in no time, it was prophesied that Atropos would choose heart failure as a mechanism to cut his thread of life.

Neha's thoughts drifted to the transient nature of relationships, which endure through time only by heavy reliance on compromise, forgiveness and perseverance. The seeds of misunderstandings were sown at an unknown hour which flourished into Blake's poison tree causing a fissure between father and daughter, which unpatched, advanced into a yawning chasm impossible to mend. Neha migrated to Australia with Prem and an unborn baby without her father's knowledge, clueless about the anguish and embarrassment such a move could spawn.

Five years later, in the wake of political changes, when Quentin Bryce was sworn in as the first female Governor General of Australia and Malcom Turnbull became the leader of the opposition, Liberal Party of Australia, efforts to conciliate were made by Vincent. Phone conversations that flowed for at least an hour, for weeks and months trickled to a halt with Vincent's condition becoming critical and his visits to the hospital. Neha recollected how towards his last days on his death bed the conversation became one sided with silence on her father's end. She could not tell if pain claimed his tongue, or a sense of disappointment coupled with the realisation that he would never see his daughter again, robbed his speech. A daughter for whom, two scores ago, he had pawned his wife's golden bangles, without her consent, to buy expensive child rearing and development books and had invested time and effort to prepare nutritious meals as 0-3 years saw the rapid development of the brain.

If she were to rummage through her memories of the innumerable sacrifices Vincent had made both for her and George, the figure would be inexhaustible. The pride in Vincent's eyes and the sparkle on his face, every time he boasted untiringly of her accomplishments and brilliance, was etched in Neha's mind never to be erased. Her sobs died out with the gradual advance of the night and she surrendered herself to snooze, the balm of woes.

ELEVEN

THORNS OF LIFE

'No, you won't,' retorted John.

'Don't you dare speak to me like that,' stated Neha, fuming with anger.

'If you had followed a study routine, you would not have scored such a pathetic mark in your test,' pointed out Neha reminding John of the heated exchanges they had had since the beginning of the year.

'How many times do I have to tell you that I had prepared for the test?' said John defensively.

'You mean you spent some time going through your book the previous evening? You wouldn't call that thorough preparation, would you? I just wish that you would stop playing Xbox One on weekdays and spend more time in meaningful pursuits,' remarked Neha nodding her head in disbelief at the spurt of rebellion.

She could not stop herself from wondering if he would have shown such defiance and insolence had he been reared in India. His attitude and behaviour was no different from any other Australian high school student and being in the teaching profession she was not entirely unfamiliar with the student culture and their perceptions that academic excellence was not the only gateway to success. Staring intensely at the fourteen-year-old shrugging his shoulders indifferently, she cogitated if he was the same boy for whom she had sought the assistance of law to ensure that justice was meted out to him six years ago. Her frustration originated from the enlightenment that the sacrifices and struggles of a single parent were beyond the comprehension of the adolescent. Either that or he simply turned a blind eye to the occurrences within the household, which was characterised by financial hardships encountered by the salaried class.

'Time for new rules. You will be allowed to go on Xbox Live only during the weekends and that too if you follow the study routine successfully. If I catch you playing on weekdays, I will lock the console up,' finished Neha with a ring of finality in her tone.

'No, you won't,' responded John.

'Watch me,' said Neha who rose from the couch, headed straight to John's room, unplugged the HDMI cable, detached the three-pin video cable connecting the console to the television and the chord from the plug point before marching forth to the boot of the car, where it was destined to gather dust for a week.

A reactionary shriek echoed in the house before it was conquered by a prolonged period of silence. Such interactions were usually followed by a patch up, a promise and a penance.

Shrieks that emanated from Neha were of a dissimilar nature. Powerless to eliminate the inequities within the school system or to avert the shocking bills despite being frugal, she often resorted to

Primal scream therapy. All the pent- up anger, stress and aggression were released in the form of unprompted and unrestrained screams to which John was a silent witness, unable to understand the magnitude of the quandary. There was a phase in her life when she financed and re-financed personal loans, increased credit card limits, and when all doors were closed due to bad credit history, pawned away jewellery and electronic goods to cope with the ever-increasing cost of living. Efforts to maintain a standard of living that befits one's profession or socio-economic class often hurled many an individual like Neha into the abyss of monetary issues from which they combated to clamber out vainly.

On that warm day in April, when she was surfing through emails she noticed that she had received one from her electricity provider. A click caused a commotion. A three-digit figure that could be rounded to a thousand rocked her sane world. Gasping in horror, she stumbled her way into John's room.

In a hysterical voice she asked, 'Can you believe this? I just received the electricity bill. How much do you think it is this time?'

'I don't know. $500 as usual?' replied John who had other concerns that claimed his immediate attention.

'$962. And I didn't even use the air con in my room. I slept with next to nothing on …,' her voice trailed off unable to pinpoint the exact cause of a high bill that was almost double the previous bill.

'You see what happens when you leave the air con on all day. During January holidays, you had it running straight for five-six hours. From now on only limited use of aircon,' commanded Neha as she stormed out of John's room.

Such unpredictable factors that hounded her one after the other denied her economic stability. Neha heaved a sigh of relief when she remembered that she would soon be earning extra income

DR. NEETHA JOSEPH

from marking operations and the much-awaited tax refunds, which temporarily mitigated her misfortunes, and made the onerous ordeal of evening out funds for the rest of the year less traumatic.

Neha reminded herself of a dialogue she had with her mother few months ago. A catch-up conversation about neighbours and relatives in India steered unexpectedly to reliable friends in Sydney.

'Don't you have any friends who would assist you when you are in a tight spot?' queried Stella with an incredulous expression on her face.

'I don't know how I am going to explain this to you. It's not that I have not initiated friendships. It just does not last,' whispered Neha.

'Nonsense. You were always surrounded by friends back home. Since when did you become such a pessimist?' questioned Stella observing every twitch on Neha's face with her sharp eyes.

'Let me put it to you this way. I befriend them and I even invite them home for lunch or dinner. And then they begin to act like they are under the spell of an evil sorcerer or sorceress and have no will of their own,' told Neha hoping that the analogy would suffice.

'What do you mean?' interrogated Stella narrowing her eyes to slits.

'Let's just say I am unlucky with friends. Friendships don't last as it used to these days. Our tendency to look for some sort of gain in the relationships is not helping either,' said Neha concluding the conversation as it was heading towards uncomfortable terrain.

Unable to resist and not wanting to let the opportunity that had presented itself slip by she continued, 'Support need not always come from friends you know. Relatives can step in too. I don't recall you or Dad or George being exactly supportive,' said Neha sharply.

'It was your choice, wasn't it? I mean you exerted your independence in every possible way. You even left for Sydney without informing us,' pointed out Stella.

90

'That's your excuse for not shouldering the responsibility of a parent? Dad did not leave me anything. You left your daughter to fend for herself all these years in a foreign country with no apprehensions of whatsoever. How convenient! Have you ever thought about my situation if I did not have this job?'

'You will get your share of the property when I die. George is a good brother and he will take care of it,' said Stella refusing to take the bait.

'What if he decides to keep it all for himself? If you are no more, I don't think I can do anything about it. It would be a good idea to take care of these things while you are alive, don't you think?'

Before the exchange could escalate into anything unpleasant, Stella left for her room immediately, complaining of a backache and expressing the need to rest for a while leaving an infuriated Neha rolling her eyes in defeat.

It was the weekend. She decided to purge all negativity from her thoughts and drown her foibles and follies in a bottle of Sparkling Rose. She selected Netflix app on her Fetch TV and sank down on to the soft couch. Ten minutes of indecisiveness ended, when she finally picked a Bollywood movie for entertainment.

Intoxication had a strange repercussion on Neha as memories of digressions plagued her euphoric mind. The gentlemen, who had the slightest impact on her straying mind, had one common tragic flaw. Cowardice. Or so she alleged. A firm conviction which rose from the similarity in occurrences. An indispensable feeling that the champagne glass would be knocked out of her hand if she were brave enough to take a sip. After a moment or two of indefiniteness, her wayward thoughts lingered on a certain Enrique Iglesias, whose semblance to the renowned performer fetched him the name. As she sat watching John clutching a swimming board clumsily and struggling to get his backstroke right at the local swimming pool, Enrique rose from the pool and approached her with water droplets sliding off his rash guard forming a trail, which continued to her seat. Neha watched him go on his knees in fascination and stared expectantly at his face uncertain which way the conversation was about to go. What he uttered was an anticlimax. A romantic gesture was wasted on discussing the slow progress of John to the next level in swimming. Captivation was replaced by rage and an appeal for a change of instructor, which was granted.

And then her thoughts rested on a non-Indian personality whom she preferred to call Antonio Banderas, not because he had any resemblance to the celebrity, but because he was an actor by profession. Although he relished Indian cuisine with gusto, loved Bollywood films and dances and enjoyed the company of Indian friends, male or female, in whose presence he mispronounced Indian words, Neha felt he lacked the nerve to try. On the parting day of a brief acquaintanceship, Antonio snapped out of his short-term amnesia and remembered the existence of a girlfriend, betraying his escapist attitude and his phobia of any relationship other than platonic. A revelation that made Neha vow that she would not have it any other way.

Neha called her next digression Jackie Chan as he was of Asian descent. A chance encounter that showed promise of developing into something profound in the initial stages. A touch that could have easily mistaken for attraction or reciprocation. A magical moment swathed in mystery. An unexplored territory harbouring unknown dangers. On an unanticipated day, Jackie Chan dropped at Neha's doorstep on a business errand and burst the dream bubble by hinting the presence of another woman in his life. It was a strange coincidence that almost all her endeavours ended with an ironic twist. Her ventures to find the much-advertised love and relationships on eHarmony failed to sustain her interest due to the intervening stages before dating and prolonged periods of wait. Unlucky with partners too, reasoned Neha.

As if she did not have enough on her plate, Neha felt the sting, the stigma of alienation, discrimination and insolence from both staff and students at her workplace for some unidentified reason. What or who was the catalyst for this unhealthy environment? A few years ago, the political manoeuvres at the school used to be of a diverse nature. Was it the move of the ruling government, who had been incriminated during the recent Federal elections of having supported dangerous racist groups? Was it initiated by the rebirth of One Nation Party with the rising popularity of Senator Pauline Hanson, whose anti-migration attacks and racist views that had ceased to shock and begun to sway more Australians to her side? Was it the creation of 'Speak English or Piss Off' Facebook page by Sydney private school students that stirred anti-Indian sentiments at school? Was it the hidden agenda provided to the principals to restructure schools, with emphasis on employing fresh graduates and downsizing, that made her feel unsettled? Was it the classic example of poor administration that required a change of leadership?

A dead end. The root cause mysterious, Neha continued to bleed from the scratches, with her futile attempts to extricate, leading to further entanglement.

TWELVE

PERQUISITION

At the knell of the bell, Year 10 students emptied out, leaving the classroom in a mess, with books strewn on Neha's table and chairs untucked. Neha picked up the worksheets and while stacking it gave a quick read noticing spelling, grammar and punctuation mistakes in most of them. She could not help agreeing with the Education Minister's attempts to raise the standards of school graduates with emphasis on literacy. Mobile phone, a necessary evil, has had a major share in interfering with the establishment of a pleasant learning environment and with the completion of classwork. As she heard a repeat of the announcement instructing staff and students to gather in the quad for the weekly assembly, she hastily stuck the pile in her drawer before she ran down the steps to reach her destination.

Confused students were figuring out their seating arrangements while Neha contemplated on how school discipline policies failed to improve behavioural patterns, when civil disobedience assumed a collective form. Neha disapproved the recent trend followed by the institution of encouraging students to move out of their timetabled classes for trivial reasons. She could not dismiss the fact that the school was indirectly responsible for the insolent and contemptuous comments that unworldly and naïve students catapulted at certain staff, insinuating that they were inefficient educators despite a decade's experience and that their popularity was fading. With the progression of each academic year, Neha felt so shackled and disenfranchised that she endeavoured to find an escape route in desperation. Unions' reluctance to represent the individual in the face of injustice and tendency to lean heavily on the institution to sort out issues, vanquished the purpose of being a union member. A realisation that led to Neha's resignation from the union.

Preoccupation with pressing concerns paved way to inattentiveness. Neha could not recall any of the announcements made during the assembly on her way back to the staffroom. Few free and a few teaching periods saw the end of the day and Neha was relieved to have survived it without any major disasters. Cruising through the peak hour traffic when she reached her neighbourhood, she heard loud voices which compelled her to take an interest in the drama that was unfolding near her dwelling. Subtle racism was still prevalent in Australian multicultural society thought Neha, who had taken the liberty to eavesdrop on the abusive language and racial insults each flung at the other. She had had her share of neighbourhood wars within few years of her migration to the country, which commenced with inconsiderate children calling out 'wog' each time she drove into the cul-de-sac to reach her residence, pulling out the calling bell from the entrance of the house, filling the mailbox with sand and stones, damaging the fence and trees bordering the property and parents supporting the children when they were caught red-handed.

One afternoon when athletics carnival had finished earlier than the scheduled time, Neha returned home early only to find children swinging at the front of the property on a tree with its widespread branches that decorated the house giving it an idyllic look. Repeated requests of asking the children not to climb on the tree had fallen on deaf ears. Neha could not comprehend why the children in the neighbourhood found that tree magnetic as their houses were populated with trees too. She knew that the tree was mutilated during her absence, for many a time when she returned, the green carpet floor on which it stood was scattered with broken branches and fresh green leaves. She was tired of polite conversations with children, who instead of rectifying their ways, chose to snigger behind her back. That afternoon she just sat in the car and honked loud and long until they descended from the tree in embarrassment, and as a parting shot, she ordered a little girl never to trespass again.

Neha let herself into the property and she was soon joined by Prem and John, who had just finished a shopping errand. Half an hour later, a knock on the door made Neha look through the French windows and the moment she saw the mother of the girl whom she had addressed earlier, she knew it was trouble.

'You stay inside. I'll handle her,' said Neha as she opened the front door to step outside.

'Why? Anything wrong?' asked Prem.

Neha was already outside speaking to the mother trying to find out the purpose of her unexpected visit.

Mrs. Hollis was a tall, attractive looking woman with blonde hair, whose face was contorted with wrath. Clad in a pale blue sleeveless cotton shirt and knee length white shorts, waving a half-smoked cigarette between her fingers, she began in a condescending tone, 'Why did you speak to my daughter? If you had any concerns you should talk to me.'

'I think you have misunderstood the situation. I was not chastising her or anything. As she was leaving the property I asked her not to trespass again,' responded Neha unhappy and furious about her patronising attitude.

'That's not what Mrs. Robinson told me. She said you were yelling at her. Don't ever speak to my daughter like that,' said Mrs. Hollis in a menacing voice, blowing a puff of smoke in her face.

Neha was unsure if the gesture was deliberate or if it was the proximity that made it seem so. She could feel the rage building within her, threatening to explode at the slightest provocation, which she was trying to suppress with an iron hand.

'Your daughter and her friends were caught climbing on the tree. They usually do this when I am at work. They are damaging the tree and it is a safety issue as well. What if they have a bad fall? There are colourless spiders on that tree,' pointed out Neha.

'The tree is not on your property. It is in the space between the mail box and the kerb, which means it belongs to the council,' finished Mrs. Hollis triumphantly, thinking that she had scored a point.

'I live on this property, which belongs to me. The council expects me to maintain that portion of the lawn as it is attached to my property. So, I am responsible for the tree as well. It's not like you don't have trees at the front of your properties. I can't believe that you are supporting the children when you know very well that they are at fault,' retorted Neha, making no attempt to conceal her flaring temper.

'I can't understand how you became a teacher. If you can't tolerate children and their actions then you need to go back to where you came from.'

All hell was let loose. The implication that being a migrant she was expected to cop the unfairness and tolerate any unjust treatment meted out to her by her white Aussie neighbours and the undercurrent of racism, unleashed Neha's fury that she had held in check.

She screamed, 'It is ironic that someone who sits at home and whiles away her time knows all about what it is to be a teacher. Let me remind you that your ancestors were once settlers or even convicts. I thought aboriginals were native Aussies and since when did you start owning the country anyway...'

Neha was unconscious of the decibel level at which she was bellowing out insults as it brought the neighbours out of their houses, who preferred to be silent witnesses to the tirade. Prem had stepped out of the house too and Neha heard him protesting when Mrs. Hollis gestured with her hand that Neha was mad and crazy. Mrs. Hollis backed off Neha's driveway, unwilling to be part of the humiliating spectacle. The heated exchange, which was tragicomic, had a profound impact on her as she became guarded in her neighbourly relations. She had very little to do with them or she kept them at bay.

It was a while ago. Changes in circumstances and in identities characterised Neha's life, which pushed back such incidents to the back of her mind. Domestic chores claimed the rest of her evening. When she retired at night she was more conscious of the functions of the chip. It was strange how one could get so accustomed to things that co-existing with it became feasible, even if it was electronic torture reflected Neha. She was still clueless about the pervert who had implanted the chip in her. She ruled out the possibility of ghosts, vampires and other supernatural beings' collaboration in ruining her disposition.

Her suspicions rested on someone she had befriended during one of the marking operations. She could not explain what had caused her to blank out while she was feeling contented in the company of a couple of friends during lunch break. She was not head over heels in love to lose track of time as she did that day. She was listening intently to a friend and could not recall when she had gazed into his brownish black eyes but the next thing she remembered was rushing to her allocated space on finding that except for them all the other markers had resumed their marking. She felt embarrassed as she replayed the incident over and over in her mind. It was as though she was mesmerised. Or did fatigue cause the black out? Was it possible for him to implant the chip in her in such a short duration? Was her other acquaintance a part of this conspiracy? If she was not an accomplice, Neha should have been informed or warned. Or was she a victim like her? What would be the offender's next move? Neha was determined not to seek help for fear of being misguided or wrongly diagnosed with a medical condition that she did not suffer from. She decided to confront the complication when it surfaced and not stress about it.

'Where to now?' Neha questioned herself. Prem had remarried and fathered two children. Did she yearn for the very mediocrities that she had fought against with all earnestness? Would she ever find bliss in the institution called marriage? It was not a case of once bitten twice shy. She was not someone who wouldn't dare to risk it all a second time. Commitments had lost its appeal. Disappointing relationships emphasised the meaninglessness of similar quests. Neha longed for something more rewarding and innovative; a venture in which she wielded power to create, to shape and to present. She turned to creative expression for solace and a new direction.

Printed in the United States
By Bookmasters